About the

Thomas Redjeb was born in Oxford and completed an MA in English at the University of Reading. He works as a primary school teacher sharing his love of writing. He has had several short pieces, poems and essays published, but *Ashbrook Manor* is his first novel.

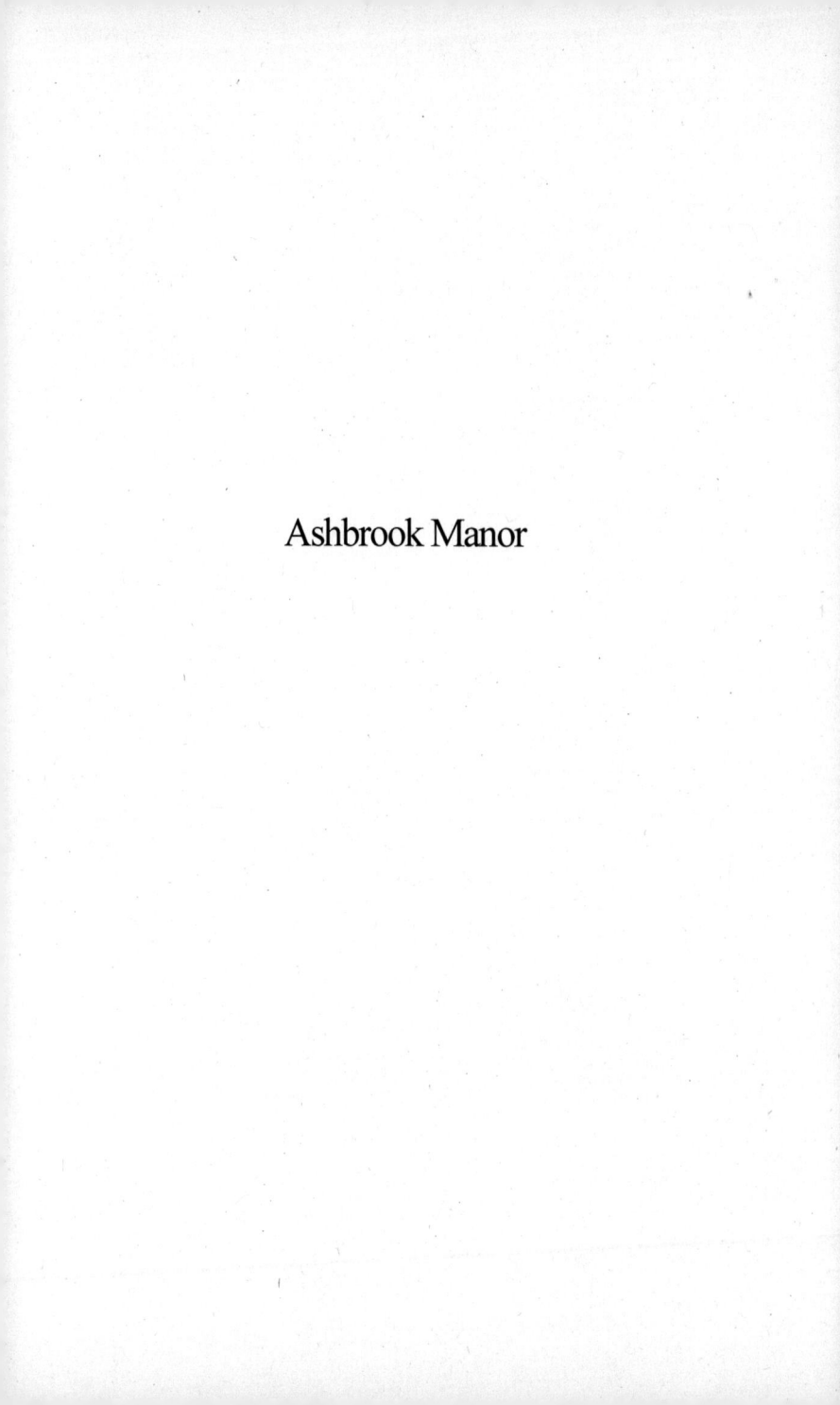

Ashbrook Manor

Thomas Redjeb

Ashbrook Manor

Vanguard Press

VANGUARD PAPERBACK

© Copyright 2025
Thomas Redjeb

The right of Thomas Redjeb to be identified as author of
this work has been asserted by him in accordance with the
Copyright, Designs and Patents Act 1988.

All Rights Reserved

No reproduction, copy or transmission of this publication
may be made without written permission.
No paragraph of this publication may be reproduced,
copied or transmitted save with the written permission of the publisher, or in
accordance with the provisions
of the Copyright Act 1956 (as amended).

Any person who commits any unauthorised act in relation to this publication may
be liable to criminal prosecution and civil claims for damages.

A CIP catalogue record for this title is available from the British Library.

ISBN 978-1-83794-622-8

This is a work of fiction. Names, characters, businesses, places, events and
incidents are either the products of the author's imagination or used in a fictitious
manner. Any resemblance to actual persons, living or dead, or actual events is
purely coincidental.

Vanguard Press is an imprint of
Pegasus Elliot Mackenzie Publishers Ltd.
www.pegasuspublishers.com

First Published in 2025

Vanguard Press
Sheraton House Castle Park
Cambridge England

Printed & Bound in Great Britain

Dedication

To my wife, my constant supporter. To my mum and dad, who have always encouraged my dreams. To my sister, who has always been there for me. To my grandfathers, who inspired me and are fondly remembered.

PROLOGUE

The curious thing about Ashbrook Manor was that no one remembered it being built. Indeed, if you asked those that lived in the neighbouring town of Melford from where it had come, they would be likely to stare at you in some bemusement before scoffing and exclaiming, 'Well, it's just always been there!'

To the residents of the town, the lavish home may as well have sprouted legs one day, uprooted itself from its original location and then laid down upon the hillside of Melford for a snooze. The appearance of the Manor was sudden, questioning about it brought upon an expression as if one was searching for the details of a hazy dream, trying to grasp at a veil of fog, and in the end conceding defeat and shrugging one's shoulders.

My first visit to Ashbrook was at the behest of my small letting firm, Brindles. I was sent along by the grouchy Mr Brindle (who, as you can see, had an ingenious naming system) after he had received a letter from the landowner wanting to sell the building which he had left vacant for some time. Why anyone would leave a manor of that grandeur empty was beyond me, but my questioning was met with blunt dismissal as Mr Brindle buried his head into a mountain of paperwork and began scribbling manically with his quill. I was sure that this was just an escape mechanism he had developed to hide from the repulsive Mrs Brindle, who was entering the shop with a list of ailments that afflicted her, a list which she recounted often and seemed to grow in size and severity every single day. I could hardly blame Mr Brindle for cowering beneath his shield of papers, yet it was futile to hide from her vicious outbursts. I remember scampering from the room just as voices were raised and the sound of slammed fists on an antique wooden table echoed throughout the building. Thus, with some haste, I had set out to evaluate the worth of Ashbrook Manor.

I strode with a brisk pace that day, for the winter was fast approaching and an icy chill hung like death within the air. Gazing up from the bottom of the hill, the Manor was an awe-inspiring sight. The brickwork was a pure, untouched white, the building spanned as far as the eye could see. Along the side of each wall were ornate windows, each with a seful stain glass design, which gleamed ever so slightly when the sun shone onto them. Despite the Manors size, it was the artistry of the craft that also brought about a sense of wonder, I was not a connoisseur of architecture by any means, but even a simpleton like myself could tell that the Manor must have been designed by one of the finest minds, for the intricate detail in every crevice, every small corner, seemed perfect. Strolling up the sheer path, enjoying the view, I couldn't help but question again why such an exquisite house had been left vacant.

After some exertion, I had neared the entrance to the Manor, two oak wooden doors adorned with golden door handles the colour of a proud lion's mane. Unlocking the door with a shimmering silver key, I walked in slowly, expecting a smell of must to overwhelm me. To my surprise, the house appeared as if brand new. The carpets lain across the entrance hall were spotless, the coatrack beside the door even appeared to have been dusted! I placed my rugged coat upon it and I remember having smiled to myself, for it was not uncommon for me to dream of owning such a place. Looking back, already I should have noticed things were not as they seemed. How would a house which had not had a living resident for some months have remained so pristinely cleaned and secondly (and more importantly), why did the house seem to resemble every dream I had ever had about owning such a Manor? I do not mean this in the casual sense, in that I would imagine a generic Manor as my own and this bore some passing resemblance. No, this was in fact, a near one-to-one recreation of the images of my own mind. Yet, I look back with hindsight (which is a wonderful thing) and recall that at that past time, as I had stood examining the Manor, that I was too overcome with pleasure at even being within the building to have noticed these finer points. However, some of the larger abnormal signs were inescapable, even for my past, deluded self. Walking into the dining room, which seemed as if to stretch on for a mile, I had come to study closer the decorative stain glass which covered each window. Stained glass was an odd choice for a window pane, as the colours and patterning would obscure the view out into Melford, and despite being in a sense of awe, I was still there to evaluate the worth of the Manor. This feature would no doubt detract from its value. Staring closer at one of the stain glass pieces, I noticed that in the bottom left corner was a figure laying in what appeared to be a bed. Taking a step backward to examine the picture as a whole, it appeared as if a whole world was laid out above the sleeping figure, as if I were staring into his absurd dream world.

'What an odd rendition.' I remember having said aloud, baffled. Studying the stained glass window directly next to this, I found it to be of the same design, yet the figure in the bed had changed. This time it was a small girl, soundly asleep, and around her another bizarre rendition of the world. It was almost as if the glass was lucid, for as I tried to focus and make out the finer details, my eyes would glaze over and dizziness would overtake me. I remember stumbling backward and falling to the floor. The hard-oak floor did not soften the blow and I landed with a particularly loud crunch. Rolling on the floor, feeling both pain and a wave of embarrassment for the absurdity of the situation unfolding, I quickly righted myself, patted my shirt and trousers and rubbed my now throbbing back before deciding I had seen enough of this room and began an ascent toward the upstairs bedrooms. Hobbling as I was, I had expected the floorboards beneath my heavy footing to creak or groan, but there was no sound. It was ghostly quiet, unnaturally so. Without a sound, I ended up on the landing. There were only two bedrooms.

Odd, I thought, as from the outside it seemed as if there would be more, but still I intended to examine what was presented before me.

Entering the first room, I was not shocked to find that there was no furniture. It seemed as if no one had ever called this place home. However, I was stunned to see that from the top corner of the room, vines had broken through the wall and were creeping down, as if reaching for me, with menacing intent. It was a blotch on the otherwise pristine nature of the home and it made me feel rather repulsed. Nature like that had no place in a home like this. Studying the other room, I found much the same, a tangle of vines drooped from the top corner of the room and were almost touching the floor. It was clear now that no one had been here for some time, as to allow overgrowth like this was not natural.

Returning outside after retrieving my coat, I hobbled around to the back of the Manor, to examine this overgrowth and was shocked to see a veritable jungle of vines had attached themselves to the back of the house, appearing as if to climb from the earth up and into the building. The owner would have to pay for this to be removed, I knew, but I felt a stirring anger within me for the lack of care given to such a beautiful home. To allow it to rot aside like this, a creation of such magnitude, seemed incomprehensible to me and I felt the owner was an ignorant, pompous fool, despite having never met the man.

Making my way slowly back to Brindles, I couldn't help

but glance back at Ashbrook. It had an enchanting quality about it – something mesmerizing. Perhaps it was simply that I knew it would remain a dream for me to own such a place, for the price point of its value I had ascertained was well beyond my meagre means. It would not be until later that I understood why I was so drawn to the Manor.

It did not take us long to draw up a simple advert, to be sent to some high earning, respectable clients, who we knew would begin a bidding frenzy over the elusive Manor. Whoever owned it was sure to be the talk of Melford and the envy of many. The advert was simple and plain, apart from a single line. Mr Brindle knew that the name alone would draw enough attention, but I had added a certain line for dramatic flair, which I felt the property deserved. It read as follows:

'Ashbrook Manor – For Sale.

The Magnificent Manor house, situated on the edge of thriving Melford town, boasts grand architectural designs, a large dining hall, two bedrooms and a splendid drawing room.

A place where dreams come true.

For inquiries, please contact Brindles, Melford, Cross Street.'

I had smiled happily reading the advertisement, pleased with my own whimsical fancy. We anticipated interest in the property, but even we could not have expected to be inundated with the number of letters we came to receive. The poor post officer, timid, frail Gerald, had to travel to and from the post office two times with a sack stuffed full of letters each time. As his bones shook like that of a skeleton, clicking and clacking as he headed back for his third trip, I felt obliged to offer my aid. The man appeared relieved, as was I at his acceptance, for I feared a third journey with a sack as full as that may well have killed the man outright. On our journey, we spoke about the Manor, and Gerald quizzed me as to the nature of the landowner. Bizarrely, I found myself unable to recall even the name of the gentleman, only that he was someone of great stature and wealth. Gerald seemed satisfied enough with this, or perhaps he was wishing to save his breath for the journey. I helped him to carry the final load of letters across the cobbled lanes of Cross Street and by the end of the trek, even my bones had begun to rattle from the sheer weight of the sack. Mr Brindle had such a toothy grin on his face as we had dropped off the final selection of letters. I had never seen him smile like that in all my time working for him. It was an unnerving pointed grin, and within his eyes I could almost make out the money that he could foresee being placed upon his desk.

'This will be the making of us my boy!' he had exclaimed with such glee. The paperwork that Mr Brindle usually hid behind was now a literal mountain, littering the floor and towering up towards the corner of his small office. Even Mrs Brindle had a hard time reaching her husband from behind the innumerable number of letters.

There were long nights ahead of us, both of us, working late into the night, by candlelight reading the letters, offers of dazzling amounts of money just for the opportunity to be the one to claim Ashbrook Manor as their own. I couldn't help but question if these people had more money than sense, as some of the amounts would have brought them a total of three Manors the size of Ashbrook.

'It's all about image my boy.' Mr Brindle had become uncharacteristically chatty since the arrival of the letters and his mood had improved tenfold. 'These posh toffs, they want the title, they don't care about the size of the Manor, or even where it is. They want the fame that comes with owning the elusive Ashbrook Manor. The press will be all over Melford like flies on dung when it gets sold, just you watch.'

Daring to ask, I remember innocently posing the question:

'Do you know who built Ashbrook? Or when it was built? The people in the town seem to have no idea.'

Mr Brindle's eyes left the letters, a rarity that he would make eye contact. His face screwed up into a tight ball, as if he were in pain. He was silent for a moment before angrily gestating.

'Who cares who built the bleeding place? Let's get it sold and earn our money boy. Wasting my time now.'

Promptly, he returned his gaze to his letters and refused to look back. It seemed as if Mr Brindle's base characteristics had not changed after all.

The winter had fully gripped Melford now, as when I left the letting firm each night the windows were thick with a layer of ice, obscuring the view from within. Indeed, the paths of Melfrod had become treacherous also, the ice seemingly covering the entire town like a blanket. Still, it was on one of these frosty winter nights that myself and Mr Brindle agreed on an offer for Ashbrook Manor.

As we composed a letter to send to the venerable Mr Highcliffe and his family to inform them we proposed to accept their offer for Ashbrook, the wind had howled furiously and the ice itself seemed to shake and shatter. For outside, in the menacing, frostbitten night dark forces were working that we could not have known or comprehended. Events had been set in motion, starting with my visit to the curious Ashbrook Manor – events which could not be stopped nor altered, as if one were trapped inside a never-ending dream.

***

I

Samantha Highcliffe was a woman of great stature, or so she had been told. Since inheriting her parents fortunes one year prior, it seemed she now had a flock of individuals who would race to inform her of her grandeur, of her beauty, of her noble heritage, yet she knew they all wanted the same thing. Money. This was why she had long ignored the sums of wealth bestowed upon her and had fled, hiding in self-imposed isolation in a small town on the American coast. It was here that she had met Randell, the flamboyant circus ringleader.

One night, in search of entertainment, she stumbled upon a circus that had set up on the edge of the town where she currently resided. It wasn't much to look out from the outside, the big tops red and white streaks were washed out, looking beiger and more muddied than anything. There were rips and tears in the fabric also, giving the impression that the circus was well travelled without ever finding much success. Still, longing for some stimulation, Samantha had entered the big top for the evening performance, along with a smattering of other folk from the town. Inside there were rickety wooden seats placed in a circle around the main ring. Placing herself delicately onto a seat, for fear it may collapse under her weight, she waited for the show to begin.

She did not have to wait long, for Randell (as she would later come to know him), in full circus garb, darted out with such ferocity into the main ring as to instantly silence the audience with his sudden appearance. His voice boomed around the tent like a lion's roar.

'Tonight, you are in for treats, delights and wonders the like of which you have never seen!'

The opening proclamation set the tone, for indeed what had started as an idle curiosity for Samantha became a fascination. Each act that followed was more enticing than that which came before, there were jugglers who threw pointed steel blades into the air with such little care or abandon Samantha could hardly bring herself to look, there was an acrobat dancing through the sky like a ballerina on a stage and just when she thought she had seen it all, a live tiger came prowling into the ring. It stalked the main circle as a tense silence fell. Each deliberate step that the beast took matched the increased beating of Samantha's heart. Its hungry eyes were scouring the crowd for its meaty supper, its jagged teeth bearing like daggers, ready to pierce the flesh. A bead of sweat ran down Samantha's face uncontrollably as the fearsome tiger came to settle in front of her. Her eyes met the beasts and saw in it only a deep, burning hunger, a desire to kill. The tiger appeared to be coiling up ready to spring at her, yet, just as it prepared to pounce, Randell, her valiant ringleader, leapt forward with such dynamism, a leather whip cracking in one hand, that he lashed at the feral beast, delivering one blow, two, three, until the creature roared in agony and retreated. As the killer crept from the ring, the crowd erupted into cheers, whoops and hollers. Randell, stood with whip in hand, his bright red troop outfit on and the dim lighting of the tent looked heroic. Samantha felt the same racing of her heart as when confronted with the tiger as she examined him. He gazed at her with a penetrating look, before returning to the centre of the ring, bowing elegantly and yelling at the top of his lungs.

'Thank you and goodnight!'

He left the arena to echoing applause and as Samantha made her way from the tent, ushered out with the rest of the crowd, there was a euphoric buzz from the group.

'I thought that lady was going to be eaten,' A voice rang out loudly.

'Never, it's just a big pussycat, I'm sure!' Called back another manly, cocksure voice.

'I'd like to see you in the ring with it!' Cried a third, followed by whoops of laughter.

Samantha was shaken, but not by her encounter with the tiger, as exhilarating as that was, but by the wave of emotion that had overcome her when observing the ringleader. Samantha had previously lived a sheltered life. Home-schooled at her parents Manor house, only allowed to play within the confines of her estate, she had never experienced some of the baser qualities of life. She had attended balls, men had danced with her and treated her with class and dignity, yet she had always longed for something which she did not quite comprehend, something which she knew existed out there, but she had not encountered until this very moment. Looking around as she entered the cold night air, she spotted the ringleader entering a small wagon. Quite overcome with emotion and seemingly not in control of her senses, she rushed over and pounded furiously on the door.

It opened quickly and the ringleader smiled at the sight of her. Without saying a word, he left the door to swing further open, tempting her to step inside. She followed and he gestured for her to take a seat on a dirty leather couch as he poured a vile-looking brown liquid into two glasses. While he did this, she scanned the room, it was filled with empty bottles, a small rail on which hung some meagre clothing and some pillows. It was certainly not what Samantha was used to and she sat rather uncomfortably on the couch, perhaps realising her mistake a little too late.

Her hero returned and slunk down beside her, callously presenting the brown liquid. While he downed his quickly, Samantha sipped the liquid, which burned her throat and made her cough and splutter.

'This stuff is quite strong for a little lady,' the ringleader said, chuckling at her discomfort before continuing, 'I just figured you could need a drink after all that.' He gestured in the vague direction of the circus tent. Finally recovering from her coughing, she placed the drink, barely touched, down at her feet and turned to face him.

'Thank you for that,' she said sincerely. The ringleader smirked.

'It's nothing, my dear. I could hardly let a beautiful lady like yourself be devoured, could I? What a waste that would be!' He seemed to have begun his ringside patter, speaking in a booming voice despite her sitting a few inches from him. 'Where are my manners though? I am Randell, the ringleader of this circus. And you are, my dear?' He moved slightly closer, the stench of sweat reeked from him, but Samantha did not find it unpleasant.

'I'm Samantha,' she replied with a smile.

'Ah Samantha. So Samantha, what brings you to a place such as this?'

His questioning set her on edge slightly, she did not want to reveal anything about her status or place within the world for fear of discovery. Yet, dressed as she was in a tatty, ragged dress and in a place like this, would he have even believed her if she had told the truth? She decided to be vague in her answer.

'I'm travelling about a bit, seeing the world. My parents recently died, so I'm finally free to do as I wish and I want.' Her words were defiant and forceful, which seemed to spark some interest in Randell, who sat forward.

'I too had parents that tried to keep me in prison, go to school, learn, get a job and support the family, but my passions lay elsewhere – the allure of the road, the joy of the theatre!' He too was speaking with some impassioned flair.

'You wanted to join the theatre?' Samantha said curiously, 'You certainly have the flair for it.'

He seemed wounded by the comment slightly as he

replied, 'Do not mock me, my dear, one day I will be a star, one day I will fulfil my dream, prove those that tread on me wrong, this is just the start for me, you wait and see.' There was some hope in his voice, which Samantha found appealing, she had never met a man with such hopes and dreams, deluded as they may be.

'I've never met someone quite like you,' Samantha offered teasingly.

'There is no one quite like me anywhere!' Randell replied joyfully, assuming it was a compliment.

Samantha retrieved her glass and with a determined gulp, swallowed the vile liquid. The burning sensation returned and she instantly felt lightheaded and warm.

'Ah, the tiger dwells within you! The fierce beating heart of a killer!' Randell exclaimed.

Samantha smiled at him as he moved closer. She did not resist, for while she had never yet experienced the joys of the flesh and had never imagined doing so in as dingy a setting as this, she was overcome with a wave of want that she had never experienced before. He clearly had some experience and took charge, removing her ragged clothing forcefully and unveiling her modesty with little pause. Outside, the dark of night shielded the lovers from prying eyes as Randell blew out the lanterns which illuminated the wagon. Indeed, as the stars lit the night sky, the pair lit something within one another, a shared experience of joy and the pleasures of the flesh, unlocking something – a feeling within Samantha which she had never dared to dream of before. The pair lay, nested in a warm embrace once the act was done, Samantha clinging to Randell's chest as he slept peacefully. She laid awake, forever changed and gazing up at the stars, which seemed just for a moment to shine brighter that night than they ever had done before. Up there, amongst them, was perhaps Randell's dream – to be star as radiant as those. The thought made her chuckle before she rested her head upon a cushion and accepted sleep's comforting embrace.

After that night, Samantha had joined the travelling circus to be near Randell and to experience a side of life which only he seemed to unlock for her. The group travelled together and over time she became accepted as one of them, the jugglers, a pair of twins that had run away from an orphanage, the acrobat, a woman who had been jilted by her lover and sought refuge from the harsh judgements of society. Even her former assailant, the mighty tiger, Smithy, came to grow fond of her petting and stroking his luscious fur. Samantha, like the others, had secrets, and much like the deep cuts on Smithy's skin from the whip, this was something each individual chose to ignore.

The one thing Samantha could not ignore though, was that the circus troupe seemed to be running out of money. She had noticed that each show drew a smaller crowd, more jeers from passers-by and in some cases incited violence from drunkards heckling.

'Go back where you came from, freaks!'

They were the outcasts of society – no home, no place to settle or call one's own. All they had was each other and even that was threatening to crumble, as each became more desperate to provide for the group that tensions arose. In turn, they all blamed one another for the failing of the group.

The only one unfazed by this bad turn of fortune was Randell, who at night spent time staring up at the stars. Samantha imagined him reaching out and trying to touch one, to cling to his dream, seemingly unaware that it was disappearing around him. Still, she had noticed that his lashings at Smithy the tiger had grown more numerous, more violent, leaving the animal soaked in blood and Randell's own hands cut from the force of the leather whip. There was a fierceness within him that both aroused and terrified her.

It was on one such night, one in which the clouds hung low and plentiful, blocking the stars from sight, that the fortunes of the group hit their lowest point. As the group slept, vandals from a nearby town slipped through the night and set the circus tent ablaze. The fire leapt into the sky, like the acrobatic dancer, it juggled its burning tips, it roared like the fearsome tiger. As the fiends fled from the scene, the group of performers awoke and rushed to the sight of the crime, but it was too late. The hungry flames had devoured the tent completely. Within the embers, the charred remains of Smithy lay, for he had been caged inside and unable to escape his fiery death. Randell was pounding the sodden earth angrily with his fists and let out a scream which shook the heavens.

Samantha watched as the juggling twins, and acrobat, each in turn, ran from the scene. That was after all what they had been doing their whole lives, running. From something, someone, or running toward a deluded dream. They had all been running in some way. Samantha knelt down in the mud beside the weeping Randell, holding him tightly to her bare breasts while he clawed at her skin.

'The dream is ruined… the dream is ruined… ruined…' He mumbled despairingly as she held him ever tighter. A dawning feeling of dread swept over her, as she knew they only had one recourse now. Later that night, when the two returned to the unsightly waggon, Samantha regaled Randell with the truth of her identity, her upbringing and the wealth in her possession if she simply returned to England. She expected a furious wrath to besiege her, but instead she was held in a warm bear-like embrace.

'My darling, my dear, my wonder!' Randell exclaimed in a state of euphoria. 'You have saved us, you have saved us entirely! The dream it lives on! Just as the stars continue to come out every night, the dream lives on!'

Samantha was not as enthused at the prospect of returning to England, for she knew the prying eyes of society would quickly return to judge her. Particularly as she would be returning with such a colourful character as Randell, who for all his charm, would not find high-society England a favourable setting.

'We shall be wed!' Randell exclaimed quite madly, 'The two of us shall be wed! Then I shall become the most grand and wonderous Lord Highcliffe, envy of the English gents and dazzler of the English women!'

Samantha was quite stunned by his sudden proposal, not quite believing her own ears. She coaxed him to bed sometime later, with plentiful liquor to calm his beating heart. She remained awake, clutching his chest, just like the first night they had made love. Yet now, as she looked out, the sky was dark, not a single star in sight. All that remained was the dark and the thick smoke from the embers of the circus tent, the embers of a life that she had made for herself and the symbol of her return to a life she had given up, not so very long ago.

***

That is largely the story of how Samantha Highcliffe returned to England. As planned, she and Randell married, he assuming her name and a lordship, she being reinstated as a woman of 'stature', Lady Highcliffe. There was much scandal and gossip upon her return and for a while the pair were plagued by newspaper reporters that were desperate to unravel the mystery of the couple. Randell loved the drama and would often play up to the cameras, loving the spectacle while Samantha would slink into the shadows, more content to hide away. The life she had ran from, one in which she was confined and safe, was now being assaulted from all sides. She desperately wished to leave her family home and in doing so was determined to sell and be done with the accursed place.

Randell was fine with this, so long as they purchased a

Manor of equal grandeur. It was as he spoke with one of the reporters one morning that he was first tempted by the prospect of Ashbrook Manor.

'Sir, is it true your up and sellin' this old place?' the reporter barked as Randell strolled back from town briskly.

'We intend to move to greener pastures yes!' Randell proclaimed, in the same booming voice which he had used in the circus tent. To him, the reporters were the same as any adoring crowd, they could be taken in by the fanciful showmanship he displayed. He was unaware that this attitude was openly mocked by both the reporters and high society.

'Any ideas where, sir?' the dirty man cried, grasping feverishly at his paper and ripped notepad, desperate for some inside scoop.

Randell smirked before dramatically exclaiming, 'Somewhere which suits the nobility of a man such as myself, of course!' He was merely bluffing here, as in fact he had no idea where his wife intended for them to dwell as he left all manners regarding money and living to her while he pranced about, visiting the finest theatres and plays he could, hoping one day to be upon the stage himself.

The reporter snivelled, 'Ashbrook Manor might suit you, sir? It's just gone on market.'

Randell was intrigued, as he had not heard of the place before, but not wanting to appear dim, he simply said, 'Ashbrook has crossed my mind yes, but is it grand enough for someone like me?'

Again, the reporter snivelled, 'It's one of the most

curious places in the whole of England, sir, right up your street no doubt.' This was meant as a snide remark, yet Randell dithered on blissfully unaware. He simply went on muttering under his breath, 'Ashbrook Manor... Ashbrook Manor...'

He presented the prospect to Samantha later that evening at supper after he had spotted the advertisement in the paper.

'This could be the place for us, my dear!' Randell said, showing her the cutting he had taken. She eyed it for a moment cautiously, as she had grown to realise her husband's suggestions were often ill thought out.

'*Hm*... it seems like it could be all right...' she stammered uncertainly. She had heard rumblings about Ashbrook Manor and had no doubt that the scandal she wished to escape would follow them there.

'My dear, it's perfect for us!' Randell proclaimed with the attitude of a child who longed for a toy in a shop window, 'Two bedrooms, perfect for visitors and a large dining hall! We could host my friends from the theatre!'

Samantha did not have the heart to tell him that those he called friends mocked him behind his back, for he was too naïve to see this. Randell was lost within his own fanciful imaginations and ramblings.

'And this is the real selling point!' He said pointing to a line in the advert. 'A place where dreams come true! Well, that's what we want, isn't it? All this time we've been chasing our dreams! Here it could come true, my dear!'

Samantha sighed and wanted to point out that it was his

dream that they pursued, she was merely a passenger to his whims now, like a battered piece of baggage. She could tell however, that he was not going to be easily swayed and perhaps after some time at Ashbrook, away from her family home, the reporters would grow tired and she would find her mind calmed. Begrudgingly, she accepted that they could send an offer to the agents. Randell planted a kiss upon her cheek quickly before pulling her to her feet and beginning to dance with her wildly. In that moment, Samantha forgot the worries of the reporters, the cost of the new home and just enjoyed life with her husband, dancing merrily and laughing at his fanciful footwork.

Thus, that very night Randell wrote to Brindles and offered an exorbitant amount of money to reside in Ashbrook Manor. As he wrote, he gazed up at the stars, through the frostbitten windows and smiled for he knew at Ashbrook his dreams would come true, believing wholeheartedly in the wording of the advert and in his own hopes. Lord and Lady Highcliffe's offer was accepted within a week and the pair set a date to move to the curious Ashbrook Manor at the start of the new year.

II

The crowd was packed tightly, dotted along the hillside leading up to Ashbrook Manor, all clambering at the chance to see the new owners of the house. Melford was a small town, but it seemed as if every individual had abandoned their daily routine to gawk at the new arrivals.

Jackson Viton rubbed his forehead gingerly as he stood waiting, the low humdrum of the crowd's chatter was giving him a throbbing headache. Viton was a reporter from the local Melford newspaper office. In fact, the town was so small, and so little happened of note, that he was the only reporter, working under the orders of the callous editor, Madame Cherrie. She had ideas of grandeur, she genuinely believed that the paper was the most important thing to Melford and that one day the office would expand. Viton was more than aware that the paper had about as much worth to the people of Melford as the toilet paper they wiped their backsides with, but he daren't argue with her for fear of losing his job. It wasn't work he enjoyed, for there was little to report on in Melford – a church service here, a funeral there, the community gathering to say a prayer for such and such. Most of their news was mere gossip and slander passed on anonymously through notes and then passed on as news at the behest of Madame Cherrie, who Viton noticed took pleasure in learning each residents' little secrets. Yet, even he had been intrigued when they heard the Brindles were selling Ashbrook Manor. He'd tried to write a piece on the place when he first arrived at Melford, but stories of its existence were so vague and hazy that he got the impression it was not worth bothering.

Still, he had caught wind of the sale through a chance encounter in the local pub with Mr Brindle himself. It had been a week earlier when, upon entering the establishment, he had spotted Mr Brindle, surrounded by a veritable crowd. It was odd as most of the townsfolk would avoid Mr Brindle if they could, the crotchety old bag would be more likely to give you an earful of venom if you came too close. Then again, if you had a wife like his, you could hardly blame him for wanting some quiet time and to find some solace at the bottom of an empty glass. On this night, though things were different, there was a crowd of vagrants sat around him, all swigging brews of different colours and textures, hanging on his every word. Motioning to remove his coat and place it upon the rack, Viton was approached by the barmaid Hannah.

'Evening, Mr Viton.' She slunk up next to him and assisted him in removing his jacket, touching him tenderly. She spoke with the tone of a sultry vixen, the words dripping with honey, that if tasted you would never escape. Viton was aware of her reputation and, so far, had kept her at arm's length, though this did not mean he was never tempted. This night, there were more interesting things at play though.

Gruffly, he replied:

'What's going on with old Mr Brindle then? The old fellas usually got about as many friends as a prickled porcupine.'

Hannah had noticed his dismissal of her approach and screwed her face up playfully.

'If you aren't going to play with me, you can go find out for yourself.'

She thrust his jacket with some force onto the coat rack by the entrance and walked away, shaking her hips seductively as she did so. Rubbing his eyes, Viton made his way over to the crowd and heckled an order over the bar for a flagon of beer.

'*Ah,* Mr Viton!' Mr Brindle had noticed his approach and singled him out. Most of the residents knew him by name and not for good reasons. Madame Cherrie's gossip mongering had not made him popular amongst the residents, a fact which was frightfully obvious as the rest of the gathered crowd eyed him with distain and were more than likely to spit on him had Mr Brindle not welcomed him in such a jovial manner. Retrieving his beer, Mr Brindle placed a bony arm around Viton and ushered him further along the bar, away from the leering eyes of the other residents. Viton could still feel their gazes, like a hawk's talons, digging into his back as Mr Brindle slumped on the far end of the counter, hiccupping. Each hiccup seemed to contort his frail bones into different, unnatural positions, which repulsed Viton so much that he placed his drink down and did not touch it again.

The old man seemed confused as to why he had even engaged Viton now as the two looked back and forward between one another. Viton decided to break the silence.

'Why are you in such good spirits Brindle? Celebrating something?'

This seemed to reinvigorate old man Brindle as he exclaimed.

'Celebrating? You bet I'm celebrating, biggest sale of my life – we're going to set for a long while, Viton and you better believe it!'

Viton couldn't help but smile, the old man's cheeriness was infectious.

'A big sale? Anything I should know about?' His journalistic side was taking hold and he could already smell the makings of a new story. Brindle's smile dropped almost as instantly as the question was asked.

'Don't you go pocking your nosey beak in Viton.' Mr Brindle jabbed a bony finger into Viton's chest, so forcefully he worried that it might snap.

'This client of mine, they want some peace, some integrity, a chance to get away from rats like you. By God, I intend to give them that,' he carried on ranting.

Viton rolled his eyes, 'Oh yes, you're certainly promoting their peace and quiet by blabbing about it to the rest of the town.' He gestured toward the rest of the group, who had begun inching closer. They could sense their chance to be rid of Viton as Brindle's attitude had changed.

'Don't you go questioning me, you young prat.' Brindle

spat as he spoke, whether this was intentional or not was unclear. His face had turned a rose red. Viton wiped the spit from his face delicately.

'Why did you even come here anyways, riling everyone up? You and that Madame Cherrie, always spreading mistruths and lies in your seedy little paper!' Mr Brindle had lost his temper now, and Viton feared that if this continued, he would end the night with broken bones as the group eagerly awaited the chance to pounce upon him.

'I shall bid you a good evening, Mr Brindle,' Viton said, and turned to retrieve his coat.

Brindle laughed hoarsely. 'Can't even stay and face an old man like me? You really are a rat!' With this proclamation, the rest of the group began to hurl insults of varying degrees of offence at Viton, who rather calmly picked his coat off the rack and began to place it on, hoping that he would get out of the pub with a bruised ego and nothing else.

Brindle was not going to let this go, however and using his clawed hands, grasped the full beer flagon that Viton had left beside him and hurled it across the room. Everyone fell silent as the liquid spilled all over Viton's jacket, soaking him, and the wooden flagon clattered to the ground with a thud beside the door. There was a tense moment, Viton felt his heart still as he eyed the group and gazed at Brindle, the old man he could easily snap in two like a twig if he wanted, and by God he wanted to at this moment. The only thing that stopped him was the cowering Hannah, an innocent in all these proceedings, crouched fearfully behind a small table in the corner. Despite her sultry nature, she had no eye for violence, it seemed. It was the sight of her that made Viton pick up the flagon silently and place it down upon a nearby table before opening the door, allowing the cold night air to blow into the pub before he uttered a final: 'Good evening.'

The harsh wind blew the door shut quickly behind him. From within, Viton heard a loud cheer and Brindle shouting that all the drinks were on him, much to the delight of the ravenous crowd. The cold beer stunk and chilled Viton as he began to walk away, scurrying back to his humble abode. However, he was stopped by a gentle hand upon his shoulder. Turning, Viton saw the face of a young man, with spectacles, he couldn't have been more than twenty, yet he didn't recognise him.

'Can I help you?' Viton blurted out angrily, not wanting to waste much time stood in the freezing air. The young man removed his hand briskly and seemed taken aback at the viciousness of the comment before bumbling:

'I just wanted to apologise for all that back there… Mr Brindle can be a right grouch when he wants…' The man was twiddling his thumbs, seemingly uncertain of himself, yet clearly, he knew of Mr Brindle.

'You know old man Brindle?' Viton asked, more calmly this time. The young chap seemed to brighten at this question.

'Oh yes, sir, I work for him! At Brindles, you know the letting agency on Cross Street?'

Viton realised this was his moment to find out some

more information about the big sale that had just occurred.

'Can you tell me why Mr Brindle is celebrating? Why is he in such a good mood?' Viton paused. 'Or was in a good mood until he saw me?' He gestured to his sodden coat with a defeated chuckle.

The young chap leaned in close and whispered, 'I feel bad for you, sir, so I'll let you know. That curious Manor, Ashbrook? Up on the hill? It's just been let, sir, for no small fee mind you!'

Viton was intrigued, Ashbrook Manor to be sold? A house of that size was likely to attract some folks of high class and pomp. Perfect for the paper.

'Do you know who is to be the new residents?' Viton pressed. The young chap cooled slightly and moved away, perhaps realising the trap Viton was leading him toward.

'I can't say, sir; the couple are extremely private and intend to keep that privacy upon their arrival next week.' At this his hands shot to his mouth. 'I've already said too much! Don't ask any more of me, sir! I shall lose my job!' With that, he scampered back into the safety of the pub, slamming the door behind him.

Viton smiled, the information he had received that night was more than enough to write a report on, and then he could be poised to learn more on the day of their arrival. He returned home that night in high spirits, but irked somewhat by his sticky coat.

The very next day he had set about informing Madame Cherrie of his discovery and the pair filled a full paper with information about the deal, speculating on who the new residents could be from their slim knowledge of high society. Still, the paper kicked up such a buzz that on the day of the arrival, the hillside was covered with residents, so much so that you would think a member of royalty was visiting. Viton held his head, regretting slightly the article, for his job would have been much simpler had there been no crowd and his head may hurt a little less. It seemed other reporters, from far more reputable papers than theirs had arrived, creating a further feverish sense of anticipation among the onlookers.

Viton sighed and decided he would make an effort to breach the frontline of the reporters, pushing past village members, who grunted and groaned as he snaked his way through the crowd. As he finally forced his way through, he was greeted by the sight of an old colleague.

'If it isn't the vulture Viton! As I live and breathe!'

Viton looked grimly over at the man, dressed in a shabby white suit, his black shirt untucked and protruding from his trousers, his tie loosely wrapped around his neck. There was no mistaking him, it was Alfie Deron, from his old newspaper office.

'Come on over here, Viton; don't leave an old pal waiting!' He opened his arms wide as if he were going to embrace him and Viton approached cautiously.

'What are you doing here Alfie?' Viton yelled so that he could be heard above the crowd. Alfie smiled leeringly.

'Why do you think I'm here? This is big news, the sale of Ashbrook Manor! No doubt some high-class toff and her husband are moving in and we want to know the ins and outs of it, my friend.' He paused and looked over at the hillside path to make sure he hadn't missed anything and when he was content, he hadn't returned to look at Viton.

'Isn't that why you're here? What paper are you with now?' he asked the question knowingly. Viton grimaced and remained silent.

'Oh, I knew it. You're with some crappy local outfit now, aren't you?' Alfie laughed heartily. 'Well, I'm surprised even they'd take you on after the stunt you pulled back with us!'

Viton gritted his teeth, he'd lost his job at his previous office due to trying to expose a member of high society. The rumour had been that the Lady of a well-off family had secretly had her parents murdered so that she could inherit the fortune. It was all gossip and hearsay, spread by the staff, but Viton had been looking into it and had a reliable source in the form of the family maid, when suddenly she disappeared. Before he had a chance to investigate further, he was removed from his position and virtually driven from the town, as the paper had run a story instead, outing him as a fraud and discrediting any of his work. That had led him to Melford, a small town where no one seemed to care what happened beyond their own little world and he had slipped back into reporting at the local paper. He had been tempted to dig deeper into his story, but the trail had gone cold, the maid had vanished, and the lady fled to another country. Where, no one knew. So, Viton had resigned himself to whiling away his life in the small town of Melford, hoping to eek out some kind of existence there.

Now, confronted by Alfie and the memory of his past indiscretions, Viton felt an urge to prove himself, a drive which had been dormant nearly a whole year. Before he could think of a remark to blast back at Alfie, he was pushed aside by the man.

'Someone's coming!' He yelled as the crowd pushed forward, almost sending people into the path of the oncoming carriage. Alfie and Viton lingered, waiting to see if they recognised the couple from within the carriage. Sadly, the curtains were drawn and all that could be made out was the shadowy outlines of a man and woman. This had not stopped the crowd surging forward and whooping and hollering. Viton's head pounded, yet he refused to give up this story, which in some way he felt was his and for some reason, he felt was his chance to redeem and prove himself.

Looking over the sea of people, he spotted a tall tree, positioned on the outskirts of the property and as quickly as he could, he began to shuffle through the crowd.

'Where are you going?' Alfie heckled after him but made no motion to follow, simply waving his hand in ignorance and turning back to face up towards the house, watching the pristine carriage trundle slowly up the hilly path toward the grand Manor. Viton meanwhile, had made his way out of the crowd and sprinted madly toward the tree.

Reaching it, he gazed up, there were plentiful branches to climb and he dug his boots into the bark, pushing himself up, higher, higher, higher, until he reached the tip of the tree. Saddling along a branch, he sat and waited, the carriage was now coming to a halt outside the Manor. By the doors he could make out the sight of Mr Brindle, his hair combed back and his best suit on, in an attempt to not look as shabby as he usually did. Beside him was the young chap who had led to all this palaver occurring by revealing the move in date, looking nervous and on edge, for he was continually removing and shining his glasses.

Then the moment came, time seemed to slow as the carriage door opened and out clambered a strange figure of man. He was tall, a towering presence to be sure, but there was something oafish about the way he stood, he didn't seem to quite fit in, as if he were playing the part of someone from high society, for his clothing was horribly mismatched, lavish colours that would have blinded you had you stared for too long. Then came the lady, she timidly stepped out of the carriage, aided by her husband. As her face came into view, Viton almost lost his grip on the branch for shock. His head became dizzy and he felt woozy. Slowly, shaking as he did so, he climbed down from the tree. Upon reaching solid ground, he slumped down at the tree stump and rested against it, clutching at his chest in an attempt to slow his beating heart. He knew that face anywhere. That was Samantha Highcliffe. That was the lady he had been investigating. That was the lady who had cost him his job.

III

Creak, creak, creak. The carriage rolled at a snail's pace up the hillside toward the Manor. Samantha and Randell were tucked inside, the curtains drawn as to hide their visage from the leering crowd. Through the thin wooden doors, they could hear the cheers and the applause that seemed to bounce around the interior endlessly. Randell could see by the sour look on his wife's face that she was not pleased. He opened his mouth to speak, but Samantha shot him such a vicious look that he quickly changed his mind.

Samantha sat, arms folded, with a stern grimace on her face. She had wanted a quiet retreat, somewhere they could get away from the prying eyes of the press and of the nosey neighbours. It seemed, despite her husband's continued promises that things were to be even worse here than at her family estate. She could contain herself no longer.

'I thought you said that we were going to make a peaceful arrival? That the letting agents were as you put it "discretion itself"?' she barked at Randell, who almost jumped in his seat.

'That's what they assured me, my dear!' He squealed like a frightened child.

'Oh yes, very discrete,' Samantha retorted mockingly, 'it

looks like the entire town has turned out! And I shouldn't be surprised if the newspapers are lined up ready to pounce.'

Randell still didn't quite understand why his wife hated the spotlight, as he relished it. He smiled slightly.

'Don't look like you're enjoying this!' Samantha cried and raised a gloved hand to strike him.

'My dear, please!' Randell yelled, gesturing to the curtains. He was sure that the audience would be able to see their shadowy outlines through the thin veil. This cooled Samantha somewhat as she returned to sulking in her leather seat for the remainder of the journey.

Finally, the carriage rolled from the hillside path and toward the Manor doors. Mr Brindle and his companion stood waiting, both fully suited and with hair well combed, as they were not used to greeting members of high society. They appeared nervous, and Mr Brindle gulped as the carriage came to a halt in front of them. Inside, Randell took a deep breath, daring to smile again at Samantha. He uttered under his breath:

'A place where dreams come true...' Before opening the door and disembarking. Mr Brindle could not hide his shock at the visage of the man. He had been expecting class and nobility, what was in front of him was something entirely else. Randell was not concerned with the men before him though, he instead had his eyes set upon the Manor, and what a Manor it was! The architecture exquisite, the size enormous – first impressions were well met. He turned back and aided Samantha down tentatively from the carriage, she still had a sour look on her face. While Randell strode backward and forward admiring the house, she moved to greet Mr Brindle and his aid.

'Are you Mr Brindle?' she asked bluntly.

He tugged at his collar uneasily. 'I am indeed Lady Highcliffe and might I say it is an honour.' He bowed his head and slapped his aid on the back, motioning for him to do the same. The two men bowed awkwardly before her.

'Spare me the pleasantries,' Samantha said, unamused, the two men shot bolt upright. 'I specifically requested privacy. Do you call this privacy?' She waved a hand in the general direction of the gathered hysterical mob, whose *oohs* and *ahhs* could still be heard floating through the air. Mr Brindle peered over at them and Samantha noticed beads of sweat forming on his forehead. His aid was staring at a rock on the ground, trying to avoid meeting her gaze.

The tension was broken by Randell's return, proclaiming:

'This is a beautiful Manor, just the kind of place for us!'

Samantha rolled her eyes as Mr Brindle rushed away from her and toward him.

'I-I'm glad it's to your liking Lord Highcliffe,' he stammered, sweating more profusely with each passing moment. Samantha moved to join her husband and linked arms with him, scanning the Manor for the first time. To her surprise, she was pleased with what she saw. The Manor was grand, it appeared like a painting, the more you starred at it, the more detail you spotted and that your eye would be drawn to a new crevice or crack for every second you spent gazing at it. She felt her unease lessen and she even smiled slightly, much to the relief of Mr Brindle.

'Are you satisfied, my lady?' he asked nervously. Samantha gave a curt nod to indicate she was, but in such a way as to impart that she had not forgotten his previous transgressions. Reaching into his shabby suit pockets, Mr Brindle produced the key to the Manor and after fumbling with it for a moment (due to his shaking hands) managed to unlock the door, welcoming Samantha and Randell into their new home. The first thing that struck them was the cleanness of the air, it was almost clearer indoors than outside. The entrance hall was expansive, boasting large decorative rugs covering the wooden panelled floor and leading toward a steep staircase. From the entranceway, the couple could just see the dining hall on the right and the drawing room entrance on the left. Mr Brindle rushed forward to take Samantha's coat, while his aid helped with Randell's.

'Have you just had this place cleaned? It's immaculate!' Randell exclaimed positively. 'We'd told the staff they'd have a heck of a job cleaning this place after you told me it was empty for so long!'

Mr Brindle smiled. 'Why yes, sir, we've had it cleaned especially for you.' His aid peered over curiously and piped up:

'But sir, we ne-ah!' Mr Brindle had delivered a quick kick to the boys shins as he spoke. Samantha raised an eyebrow, looking over at the two. Mr Brindle laughed nervously.

'What the boy means...' he began and Samantha was quite keen to hear the end of the sentence, for it appeared from the look on Mr Brindle's face he was just as unsure as she was of where the thought would end up. '... is we only managed to get the cleaners in short notice, we weren't with them, no. But we did get them in.' He turned to face his companion and smiled before, through gritted teeth, uttering, 'Didn't we boy?'

His companion grew weary and red faced, nodding meekly. Samantha noticed and glanced pitifully at the young chap, who was once again staring at the ground. Mr Brindle raced forward to lead them on a tour of the Manor. Firstly, into the drawing room, which consisted of a cushioned sofa and fireplace with some wooden logs inside it. It was spacious enough, and Samantha grew weary at the thought of the gatherings that her husband would undoubtedly conduct here. Moving toward the window pane to peer out and check if the crowd was still present, Samantha noticed for the first time the stain glass panes, which comprised of all the windows in the Manor. Randell was deep in conversation with Mr Brindle, regaling him with a tale about when two playwrights had visited their previous home. Mr Brindle hung on each word greedily and Samantha got the impression these stories would be passed onto the village folk later that very day. Samantha returned her attention to the intricate stain glass windows, their vivid colours obscuring vision into the outside, casting the crowd outside as streaks of black rather than people. Placing a hand upon the glass, she found it cold to the touch and she recoiled slightly, drawing her hand in close to warm it.

Once Randell had finished his tale, they were led into the dining hall, which did indeed seem to stretch out for a mile. Randell quickly dismissed the room, he was more interested in the food and who he could invite to dinner rather than where he ate it. He pulled Mr Brindle aside as they strode into the entranceway, questioning him on the local theatres and other playwrights of note. Samantha lingered, taken in by the sight of the stain glass. As she looked from further away, she could make out the depictions of various people sleeping with what appeared to be variations of the world above them. Some were bright, colourful and welcoming, while others were nightmarish, almost beyond comprehension. Behind her, Samantha noticed Mr Brindle's aid lingering.

'Do you know something about these?' she asked, genuinely curious. The young man moved forward rubbing his glasses with his fingers.

'I don't really – I just noticed them when I was last here.' Samantha gave him a quizzical look, but it was honestly answered, 'I came here to value the property you see.'

Samantha smirked. 'So it was you who wrote that fanciful advert then?'

The young man looked puzzled, 'Fanciful miss? How so?'

Samantha rolled her eyes before grinning mockingly, 'A place where all your dreams come true. That part of the advert is what convinced my husband to put an offer on this place. He's always been a bit of a dreamer, you see. In fact, he'll probably commission one of these awful things that shows him dreaming!'

The young man didn't appear to approve of her mocking tone replying, 'Everyone's got to have a dream miss, it's what gets us up in the morning and keeps us going. Without dreams, where would we be?' He was staring off into some fanciful daydream as he spoke. Samantha couldn't help but admire the naïve optimism in the way he spoke. He was young. So was she. But things change.

Not wanting to wound his spirits, she patted his shoulder gently, 'You keep on dreaming,' she said, before leaving the room, while the paintings kept on sleeping.

The group went upstairs next and were shown the two modest bedrooms, Randell was particularly irked to find the vines that he had been promised would be removed were still very much intact in each bedroom.

'What do you call this ey Brindle?' he blurted out, losing his composure momentarily. Samantha placed a hand calmingly on his back, their roles having reversed from the start of the day.

'Can we arrange for these to be removed please? We can hardly sleep in here with all this flora about,' Mr Brindle explained that the town was so small it only had one gardener and he was recovering from a nasty fall.

'He'll be right as rain soon and over before the end of the week,' Mr Brindle assured them.

'You make sure he is,' Randell scoffed. As Mr Brindle and the young boy walked ahead, Samantha whispered to her husband.

'What's wrong with sleeping on the sofa for a few nights? You never used to mind.' She smiled, reminiscing on the days in which she and Randell would fornicate wildly on that shabby old sofa. While a seedy memory to others, to her it brought great comfort and would remind her of why she was still with Randell now.

Randell winced as if in pain and retorted, 'That was when I was a ringleader and you no more than a peasant. Now I'm a man of class, you are my Lady. We should expect the finer things from life. We have earned them after all.'

Samantha wanted to tell him they had earned nothing but felt such a comment would only provoke further anger, so simply nodded along as they returned to the entrance of the Manor.

'Well. This is yours now, I believe Lord Highcliffe.' Mr Brindle handed the key over to Randell obediently. Randell nodded in approval. 'Please if you need anything… anything at all, we are just down in the town at Brindles. On Cross Street.' He rambled.

'We know where to find you,' Randell said dismissively. Samantha waved courteously to the young man, who smiled and returned the wave with a simple, uncouth bow. The two disappeared down the hill, blending into the crowd as they no doubt descended upon them to receive the latest gossip. Randell slammed the door shut and turned to face his wife.

'Alone at last, my dear, in our new home nonetheless.' He seemed pleased with himself and paraded around the entrance hall, taking in the sights like a strutting peacock.

'We have this whole night to ourselves, my dear. The staff won't arrive until tomorrow morning, along with our other belongings.' He was smiling to himself, teasingly. 'You talking about the old days has ignited a passion within me.'

Samantha coyly strode into the drawing room, disrobing as she did so. Randell chased keenly after her as the stain glass paintings watched over the two lovers.

Later that evening, Randell managed to get a fire started using the logs and lanterns that had been left by Mr Brindle. He picked up and wrapped a rug around his bare wife, who lay sound asleep on the wooden panelled floor. She must have been quite exhausted after their arduous journey, for he knew how she fretted when under public scrutiny. Picking her up, he placed her onto the sofa and lay beside her, his head resting close to hers. The warmth of the fire, her body heat and the rug lulled Randell into a drowsy state and he soon found himself unable to resist the urge to close his eyes and sleep. As the two figures lay, huddled together in a loving embrace, sound asleep, they were unaware of the shadowy streak pressed menacingly up against the stain glass window, watching their every move from outside in the cold, restless night.

IV

Viton stumbled back to the office in a haze. He still couldn't quite believe what he had seen, and yet he had seen her with such clarity there was no mistaking it. Samantha Highcliffe. The name burned into every crack and recess of his brain, like a record stuck on repeat, the name spun and spun around in his mind until he thought he might faint. Clutching his head, he slunk into his uncomfortable chair as he entered the small office space.

The room was tiny and could just barely fit the two desks, which made up the entire assets of the Melford Gazette. Viton believed you could tell a lot about a person from their desk. His was neat and ordered, methodical and cold. Madame Cherrie's, however was a cluster of papers, post-it notes, pens and doodles carved into the wood. In their quietest moments, Viton would often glance over and see Cherrie digging into the desk with a small pocket knife, creating what she called 'art', but he called vandalism. Now, in his heightened state the furniture, the walls, the floor – all of it seemed to be spinning, veering wildly and with increasing speed in front of his eyes. He found no relief in closing his eyes, for the black void itself appeared to be turning, like an object being sucked into a tornado wildly.

As his vision began to blur and he felt his head drooping toward his shoulder, in the chaos he could make out a feminine figure coming toward him calling his name.

'Viton… Viton…' the voice faded as all went dark.

Suddenly, jolting awake, Viton came face to face with Madame Cherrie, who was lingering uncomfortably close to his face.

'Bloody hell!' she exclaimed, recoiling slightly as he awoke, leaning back and resting on his desk in an effort to compose herself. Viton saw she was wearing her usual tight-fitting blue suit trousers and a jacket. She had told him she wore these to seem more respectable and business-like, unaware that she, like the paper, was mocked and ridiculed for this approach. Her face was wrinkled and carried with it the scars of a lifetime of disappointments, hidden by her mask of unflinching optimism that just one good story would put them on the map. Now, her face was slightly reddened by her outburst and catching her breath, she uttered, 'Sorry you scared me.'

Viton rubbed his temples, the headache was receding, but the pain lingered slightly.

'What happened to you?' Cherrie questioned intensely – too intensely for someone who had just passed out. 'You look like shit.' Again, straight to the point.

'Thanks for that.' Viton shot back bluntly, but did not answer her first question.

Cherrie waited, staring expectantly. Viton instead deflected by asking:

'Do we have anything to drink?'

Cherrie scoffed, 'Drinking on the clock? That's not what I pay you for.'

Viton grimaced, 'I did just pass out.'

Cherrie rescinded and went to her desk, digging out a bottle of clear liquid from under the piles of papers. She may have been intense and demanding, but she wasn't heartless. Catching a glimpse of himself in a small mirror that hung on the wall, he realised why she was so concerned. His face had a haunted look to it, pale and somehow gaunter than it had been at the start of the day. His eyes, bloodshot and red raw, appeared deeply saddened.

Returning with a small glass of the clear liquid Viton grasped it quickly and swallowed it all before coughing and spluttering viciously.

'I was going to warn you, it's quite strong,' Cherrie said, she almost laughed, but seeming his clear discomfort, she held the chuckles back.

'What is that? Petrol?' Viton managed to splutter through the coughing.

Cherrie shrugged. 'Who knows? It's been on my desk for an age.'

Viton managed to regain control of his lungs. If Samantha Highcliffe didn't kill him, Cherrie's alcohol certainly would. There was the name again, ricocheting through his mind, infesting each and every thought.

Cherrie grew impatient of tending for Viton, she knew that the biggest story their humble paper would get was on her doorstep and was eager to find out more.

'So go on, tell me. Did you manage to see who has bought the house?'

Viton paused for a moment, unsure of whether to tell her. She would find out eventually of course, it would only be a matter of time before the town was abuzz with the news. In the end, he decided to repay the ounce of kindness she had shown him with the information.

'Yeah, I did, Samantha Highcliffe and her new husband. They're the two who have bought the house.' The words hung in the air, poisonous to Viton but like sweet nectar to Cherrie. Her eyes had lit up like lightbulbs. She clapped her hands together and began to mumble incoherently to herself. Viton caught the occasional word:

'Better than we'd hoped... This is real news... those two are scandalous right now...'

Viton coughed and Cherrie turned to face him, as if she had forgotten he was there.

'This is great news Viton!' she exclaimed passionately. 'This story is really going to make us. Those two have so much dirt on them, surely you've heard of them?'

Viton nodded, trying to appear aloof in his response: 'Bits and pieces yeah.'

Cherrie almost squealed, 'Oh yes, those two are as scandalous as they come. High society hates them, the paupers love their seedy drama. This will be great for us, mark my words!'

Unenthused, Viton buried his head in his hands. Cherrie

came over and grasped his shoulders firmly, shaking him.

'Come on Viton! I need you at your best here! Our first big story since you got here comes knocking and you're slacking off! I can't, no, I won't have it!' Viton looked up, bleary-eyed. Her face appeared to have lost ten years of age through pure excitement alone, like a child let loose in their favourite sweet shop. Feeling a skin crawling urge to escape her grasp, Viton put on his best smile and nodded along.

'I won't let you down. In fact, I'll get out there right now.' He proclaimed, shaking off her grip, but wobbling as he stood up, his legs noodles beneath him. Cherrie looked a little concerned that she was sending her only employee off when he was clearly unwell, but her desire for the story came first.

'I'd head over to Brindles if I were you,' she said, 'the old man was up there showing the two of them in, no doubt he'll happily recount his tale for you.'

Viton sighed, he hadn't told her that his last exchange with Mr Brindle hadn't ended on the best of terms, he'd only given her the information about the move, skilfully leaving out the soaking he had received as to keep some semblance of dignity. Recalling the night, he suddenly had an idea. The young chap who worked with him, that had shown him some kindness, perhaps he could ask him for some information, for surely, he had been up there to see the new couple in?

Viton picked up his jacket and wrapped it around himself. Cherrie gazed down the long hallway which lead to their office as Viton took each calculated step as not to lose his balance. After some effort, he reached the door and Cherrie called out:

'Good luck Jack!' In a genuinely concerned manner. Viton did not hear her, for he was already out of the door, ready to prowl the packed streets in search of information.

***

Viton was glad to be out in the cool breeze, clearing the stifled air of the office from his lungs. As he walked slowly out into the street, his mind continued to race. Why had he passed out? Fear? A panic attack? Perhaps it was the fact that the peaceful, boring life he had carved out for himself was all but certain to cave in. He wasn't sure he could face moving and starting again, yet the haunting, spectral figure of Samantha Highcliffe lingered in his brain, clouding his judgement, ready to strangle the life out of his newfound existence, just as she had so quickly ended his prior life. Uncertainty stalked his every move, half of his brain telling him to flee and not return, the other half, a dogged, rough, beaten part of the brain, the part which had simply had enough of the torment, was telling him to stand up and fight for his life. To be free of the dreaded Samantha Highcliffe for good.

Making his way to Cross Street, Viton had to navigate a veritable sea of people. Whoever had designed the pathways and narrow roads of Melford had clearly never envisaged such crowds, for everyone walked in at an uncomfortably close distance, which made worse for Viton as his legs were still very much out of his control. Every so often he would veer limply into the stranger walking next to him, and he would be forced to mumble some kind of grovelled apology. He was cast aside with general grunts of discontentment. It was clear that the crowd was following someone, a pair of figures at the forefront of the street and as they reached the humble Brindles, Viton had figured out that the crowd were traipsing after the old fellow, trying to distil some gossip from him, no doubt. Finally, the crowd came to a halt, forming a huge horseshoe shape around the front door of the lacklustre shop and over the lull of the crowd, Viton could make out Mr Brindle's dreary tone, conveying a message to the people. Surging forward like an unstoppable wave, Viton pushed and shoved, ducked and weaved, until he was near the front of the group. Beside Mr Brindle stood the young man, almost timidly cowering behind him. When he peered up at the crowd, he caught Viton's eye as he hoped he would. Gesturing with his hand, Viton slipped into a dingey alleyway beside the letting agents, hoping the aid would follow. After a few moments of suspenseful wait, he stumbled around the corner, Viton grabbing him and pulling him into the shadows so they could not be seen by the predatory crowd.

'Get your hands off me!' The young man cried, as if he were being mugged, shoving his hands weakly into Viton.

In his diminished state, Viton lacked the strength to hold him and fell backward against the harsh brick walls. Shocked at his own actions, the young chap came forward to help him, but Viton waved his hands away.

'I don't want to hurt you,' Viton said gruffly, 'I'm just trying to keep you hidden from the crowd.' He dusted off his coat and pointed at the light peering into the alleyway entrance.

The young man's face lit up. 'You're the chap from the pub! The one Mr Brindle had a falling out with!'

Viton nodded glumly, for he didn't need reminding of the events. Uncaringly, the man continued:

'You've still got that beer stain on your coat!' He pointed at the faded marks on the side of the jacket. It was true, Viton had struggled for some time to remove the markings, which proved to be more persistent than he had imagined. In the end, he had simply given up.

'All right! All right!' Viton said loudly, wiping the look of glee from the man's face. 'I don't need reminding.' He sighed, collecting himself before saying. 'We've got off on the wrong foot here. I'm Jackson, Jackson Viton.' He paused. 'And you are?'

The young man looked concerned and twiddled his thumbs before answering apprehensively, 'My name is Lee, Lee Mallet.'

'Nice to meet you Lee.' Viton extended a hand, expecting it to be shaken. Instead he was it was left hanging, awkwardly. Lee eyed it fearfully.

'You're Jackson Viton with the newspaper, aren't you?' Lee said cautiously.

Viton knew there was little point hiding it and simply nodded in response.

'Mr Brindle warned me about you, sir. Said you'd come sticking your nose into Lord and Lady Highcliffe's busi—' A hand shot over his mouth. 'I've said too much already, sir! Mr Brindle will kill me!' Lee was clearly despairing as his eyes widened and a pale fear washed over his face. Lee turned to flee, to escape from the shadowy alleyway, but Viton was ready and quickly pounced, pinning him to the wall with more force, adrenaline fuelling his body and restoring some of his strength. Lee was a timid, weak man, and Viton had the upper hand this time.

'Help! Help me!' Lee cried out desperately, but in the darkened corner of the alleyway and with the crowd roaring outside Brindles, his cries went unheard and unanswered. Viton placed a sweaty palm over Lee's mouth.

'Don't speak. Don't move. Just listen,' Viton said in a low, but threatening grumble. Lee became limp, but Viton did not remove his iron-tight grip. 'I want to know all you know about Lady Highcliffe. I want to know everything about that house – who owns it. I want to know it all. And you're going to give it to me.' He paused, allowing the ferocity with which the words were said to sink in. They had the intended effect as Lee's eyes welled up fearfully. 'Do you understand?' Viton snarled like an animal, feral and ready to be let off the leash.

Lee nodded, and a tear fell uncontrollably down his cheek. Viton loosened his grip and removed his hand, the force with which he had been holding him had left red indents in his face.

'I don't know that much…' Lee blurted out, finally able to draw breath and rubbing the tears from his cheeks. Viton moved to grab him again, but Lee recoiled and shouted, 'Wait! Wait!' causing Viton to pause, his hands still outstretched, as if ready to attack at a moment's notice.

'Mr Brindle, he has all the paperwork, from the pair of them and the man who was selling the place…' Lee blurted out quickly, 'he won't let you have those though…'

Viton sneered. 'But you could get them, couldn't you?'

Lee's eyes darted around as if looking for an escape and quickly froze when he realised there was nowhere to go.

'I… I can get you them yes…' Lee sighed.

Viton smiled 'Good. Meet me here tomorrow night then.' Viton strolled to the end of the alleyway contently before turning back to face the shell of a man. 'With the papers Lee. Or else.' The threat was thinly veiled and had the desired effect as Lee nodded frantically. Viton left him there, trembling in the shadows.

An evening dusk had settled over the town of Melford, a blood red sun lowering behind the skyline. Viton walked with renewed vigour, moving away from the crowded Cross Street and heading home. A chill was slowly encroaching upon the town, but Viton felt raging heat burning within him. A passion which had been remained unkindled until today. This time things would be different, he assured himself as he walked. This time, he would bring down Samantha Highcliffe. Whatever it took.

V

Samantha clasped her husband closely as a chime rang out through the Manor, echoing around the large, empty rooms ominously. The fire that was lit in the drawing room was nothing more than smouldering embers now, with small puffs of smoke floating from the fireplace, thus the room had become a frozen tundra. Shivering, Samantha clutched at the rug, which was half hanging off her body, in an attempt to keep warm as the chime continued to ring out. She endured listening to its dull tones for a few moments more before attempting to rouse Randell so that they may seek out the source of the disturbance.

She shook him, gently at first but then more forcefully, but whatever she did he wouldn't stir. With a tut of disapproval, Samantha got up and retrieved her clothing in an effort to stop herself shivering. After dressing, she glanced out of the window, it was pitch black, with only the light of the pale moon illuminating the house. She had hoped that the incessant chiming would have stopped of its own accord, sadly she was proven wrong as it continued to ring out. It seemed to her to be originating from one of the bedrooms upstairs, which was odd as she hadn't recalled seeing any kind of clock on their tour around. Still, presuming she had simply overlooked it, Samantha began to edge her way out of the drawing room and toward the staircase, running her fingertips along the wooden walls to help guide her down the darkened hallways.

Fumbling her way along the corridor, she finally reached the staircase and began to ascend, with each step the chime ringing out louder and louder. She was a woman of a level-headed nature, but even she had to admit this was unnatural, and her mind began to race with inane possibilities as her heart began to beat irregularly. Still, she ascended, as if on autopilot, and came to rest at the top of the staircase. Peering into one of the bedrooms, she could see no clock or source of the chime, yet it was still becoming louder with each passing moment. Darkness had nearly overtaken this room, and the blackness, like a yawning chasm, made Samantha tremble with trepidation. Waiting in the doorframe for a moment, she hoped her eyes would adjust to the thick blackness, yet it seemed to be infinite and unknowable, for after a few moments she could not make out any more of the room's details. She had half a mind to turn back, return to the warm embrace of her husband and try to cast aside the chime. By morning, the source could be found in the safety of daylight. But the chiming had clawed into her mind, digging in deeply and she knew she would not rest until it was found. Taking a deep breath, Samantha entered timidly, feeling her way around the shadows slowly.

Her fingertips ran along the cold, smooth wood as she edged around the room, searching for the chime. Suddenly, she let out a gasp as her hands touched the overgrown vines that had protruded into the room. The change in sensation had shocked her, but remembering that she had seen the plant life earlier that day calmed her nerves. Pushing onwards, she ran her hands through the dangling vines, the leaves twisting around her hands and wrists sensitively. They clung to her and seemed to want her to stay as they desperately wrapped around her, but Samantha, intoxicated by the allure of the chime, pushed on and cast the vines aside.

Strangely, she came to feel the frame of a second door. Yet she knew that from their tour that there was no other door, and glancing back, she could make out the doorframe from which she entered the bedroom illuminated by the moon's white beams. Running her hands over the door, she could feel the intricate design emblazoned upon it, but in the all-consuming darkness could not make out what it was supposed to depict. Splinters of jagged wood poked out of various areas of the door, pricking Samantha's delicate hands. She felt the bubbling of her blood as the small cuts revealed the scarlet liquid under her skin. Rubbing her aching hands, she placed an ear to the door. From behind it came the continued, unmistakable chime. Searching for a moment, she found it. The door handle, metallic, icy to the touch in the cold nights air and stiff as Samantha pressed down on it. Her cuts poured droplets of blood over the handle as she used both hands to force the handle downward, finally managing to drag the door (which was surprisingly heavy) open a fraction.

A radiant light poured from within, shooting outward into the bedroom. Samantha, enthralled by the sight, pocked her head around the door, using one eye to peer through the crevice she had opened. Samantha could not ever fully describe what she saw within that room. The first thing she noticed was the colours dancing around the air, filling the room with light, the next macabre figures gathered around the bedside of what looked like a young girl. Each figure was no more than a shadow, observing her sleep, yet they did not touch her. Rather they watched, a dozen figures or so, hazy shadows flickering under the multi-coloured spectral lights as the girl, tucked up under a thick duvet, slept soundly. She appeared to sleep peacefully, despite the technicolour show above her, the figures surrounding her, and the now deafening chimes of the clock, which Samantha could see at the far side of the room. It was a grandfather clock, bronzed and antique looking, its gears and pendulum on view, swinging back and forth hypnotizingly. Samantha was astounded and bewildered at the sights, and she felt her mind slipping beyond the realms of sanity as the room twisted, distorted, and spun before her. The very ground that made up the room seemed to be disappearing, slowly becoming translucent. It was as her head spun and she felt she were being thrown around in a spinning hurricane that one of the shadowy figures seemed to note her presence. It moved unnaturally toward her, lurching over wildly as if it had no bones at all but not making a sound. Samantha felt her heart pound, a wave of terror washing over her the likes of which she had never felt before, she was sweating profusely as her temperature skyrocketed and she felt lightheaded. Trembling, the haunting figure reached the doorway, and Samantha felt her eyes fill with water, tears of fear threatening to fall at any moment.

Boom! The door slammed violently and Samantha was blown back across the room by an unseen force. She lay, sprawled out on the hard bedroom floor, unable to get up as her body convulsed in both pain and horror. The chimes of the grandfather clock were dimming, slowly fading as if getting further and further away. Slowly, Samantha's eyes fell shut as she could stay conscious no longer.

It felt like a lifetime later that his eyes fluttered open. The sun was streaming through the stain glass windows, the birds chirping, signalling the start of a brand-new day. The frost which had covered the windows was slowly melting, forming water droplets that flowed slowly down the window panes. To her surprise, Randell was next to her, the two of them still in the drawing room, still bare beneath the rug. She couldn't remember having returned down here. Clambering over Randell's lumbering form, she raced back upstairs, not stopping to dress, and shot up the staircase and into the bedroom.

Fully lit by the sun's assuring glances, the room seemed less hostile, but the door through which Samantha had witnessed the strange vision was gone. Replaced by a smooth wooden wall that covered the rest of the room. Samantha neared the spot where it had been and touched it sensitively.

She tried to recall the details of the previous night's events, but the more she attempted to focus on them, the more the memories became a haze, like staring at a picture with the wrong glasses, a blur. From downstairs she heard Randell stirring, and she hastened to his side, keen to be away from the peculiar room.

As she entered the drawing room, he was sat on the sofa, rubbing his head. She stood before him, he looked up at her with a smile.

'My dear, you'll catch a chill walking around like that,' he said, reminding Samantha of her nakedness, as she scurried to dress herself.

'Besides, the staff will be here soon, with all of our things,' he mumbled, retrieving his own clothing as he spoke and discarding the rug.

Samantha remained silent and Randell could tell something was bothering her.

'Are you okay, my dear?' he asked, moving and placing his warm hands upon her shoulders as she had her back turned to face away from him.

'Did you hear a chiming last night?' she asked coldly.

Randell appeared to give it a moment's thought before replying. 'I can't say I did, but then I was out like a light, sparko.' He peered round at her pale face, noticing the large shadowy bags under her bloodshot eyes. 'Did something keep you awake then?' he asked, genuinely concerned.

Samantha gazed out of the window, seeing the carriages full of their belongings coming into view at the bottom of the path. She also saw the crowds of individuals, once again flocking for a look, for some insight into the lives of the owners of Ashbrook Manor. It seemed from each side she was assaulted. She knew she couldn't explain the previous night's events, in fact, she was now uncertain if they had even occurred, perhaps they were simply a stress-induced dream.

Randell could see from the troubled expression on his wife's face that something disturbed her, but he also knew she would come to explain it in her own time and that it was not worth prying. Instead, she spun her around to face him and beaming he said.

'My dear, this is our fresh start – a chance to find a place to call home. If we give it a couple of days, the mongrels will tire of their pursuits and leave us be, then you can be free of their torment. Then our dreams can come true.' He paused to check she was listening. Her face was half glazed over, but he carried on regardless. 'I'll find work at the theatre, we'll host the most lavish parties, you'll see, we'll find fame and fortune.'

Samantha seemed to take note of this and shot back. 'We already have fortune. My parents saw to that. We also have fame, but for all the wrong reasons.' She despaired.

'But soon, very soon, they will be the right reasons!' Randell insisted, clasping her hands in his. 'Just you wait, my dear. I'll make you proud.' He kissed her forehead affectionately as a knocking on the front door rang through the halls.

'Lots to do!' Randell smiled, racing to the doorway.

'First things first, we make this our home.' He said, with the enthusiasm and vigour of a man ten years younger, before disappearing to answer the front door.

Samantha lingered, hearing him greet the staff in the distance. She returned to the window, peering out through the vibrant panes at the gathering crowd below. As she placed her hand tentatively on the window, she saw the bloodied cuts still oozing and fresh from the night before.

VI

Viton woke slowly the next morning, his head still groggy from the previous day. He rolled over meekly and reached for his watch, pulling it from the basic bedside table. It was just after nine am, and he knew he'd have to head back over to Ashbrook today, as he was sure a crowd would gather to see the carriages full of ludicrously expensive furniture arrive. He aimed to use this as his chance to creep onto the grounds, unguarded by a fence or walls, and try to speak to one of the new staff members arriving. They would be able to uncover some of the details around Samantha Highcliffe's sudden re-emergence, he was sure. Besides, he had time to kill before he met up with Lee, whom he hoped would deliver him the documents.

Getting up slowly, he manoeuvred into the kitchen. His flat was small, with three rooms, a kitchen, a living room (turned bedroom) and a bathroom. Every morning his routine was the same, finesse himself around the edge of his bedding in the centre of the room to reach the thin kitchen, drink a mug of coffee and then shower before heading out. He was a creature of habit and as he poured himself a cup of the steaming liquid, his mind wandered back to the events of the previous day. Samantha Highcliffe returning had a profound effect on him, the meek existence he had carved out in Melford was in question and reflecting, he found himself shaken as to the lengths he had gone. He wasn't a confrontational man, nor a violent one, at least he didn't think. Yet as he stared into the black liquid filling the mug, all he could see was the terrified face of poor Lee, a man who had once comforted him, now reduced to a fearful wreck, at Viton's hands. Picking up his cup, he trembled slightly at the thought, scolding his bare feet with the hot liquid, pulling him violently back into the present. Shaking his head and cleaning the floor and his feet, he decided to cast the memory from mind, all that mattered was exposing Samantha Highcliffe. He had time for humanity later.

***

An hour had passed by the time Viton reached the hillside of Ashbrook Manor and swathes of people had already started to form as the first of several carriages came rolling by steadily. Viton scoffed, the items inside were extravagant and garish, of that he had little doubt. Just the sort of materialistic goods that people like him and the rest of the town could only dream of owning. He was repulsed by the adoration the crowd showed, but he knew that deep down it was an inadequacy with their own lives that lead them to heaping praise upon two individuals they didn't even know, purely because of their wealth and status.

Standing for a while amongst the preying vultures, Viton

waited until the first carriage reached the Manor before he began to ascend the hillside, slinking his way around to the back of the Manor. Kneeling behind the shrubbery to remain out of sight, he dared to glance up at the house and get a view of the comings and goings of the staff. What caught his eye immediately was the unsightly greenery growing over the back of the Manor, its vines and tendrils creeping into every orifice. It had not escaped the attention of the staff, who's service entrance was mere feet away from the natural monstrosity. Two men, dressed in white shirt and black tie, stood, pointing and gesticulating at the overgrowth, no doubt complaining. Viton imagined that the staff had expected a house of quality and class, and indeed, Viton himself found he valued the house less after seeing the unseemly roots. As the two men disappeared into the service door, Viton remembered why he was there. He needed to find someone young, inexperienced, perhaps a new hiring, for it would be easier to deceive them. The more experienced staff would surely be able to suss out his plans immediately.

The opportunity he had been waiting for presented itself more quickly than he had imagined, for he spied rounding the corner of the house a youthful girl, in her maid's uniform, carrying bags, full of clothing no doubt. As she walked around toward the service entrance, Viton crept from behind the bushes. A stroke of luck caused one of the bags to split and clothing to spill out onto the dusty ground and while the girl was distracted, Viton made his way over unnoticed.

'Can I help with that?' he asked as he approached. The

girl looked up shyly but clearly shocked by his sudden appearance. She nodded timidly as he began to pick up the assorted scarves that littered the floor. The pair worked silently for a short while, the girl glancing at Viton occasionally, he risking a glance around to make sure no one else was about. He knew he would have to try to work quickly.

'I'm Lee,' he said coolly, for a false identity never hurt anyone.

The girl paused what she was doing and brushed the maroon hair, which hung low over her eyes, out of her face before replying, 'I'm Jessica.'

Viton smiled as sincerely as he could and told her it was nice to meet her. The two continued to place the items back into the remaining bags and Viton commented:

'The Lady has a lot of things.'

Jessica took the bait and replied, 'The Lady is very well off.' There was an air of bitterness to the response that Viton seized on.

'Do you know her well?' he asked honestly.

Jessica rolled her eyes, her face displaying teenage angst. 'I've only been with her a while, but she gets me to do all sorts of rubbish jobs. Changing her linens, vacuuming, even making her bed!' The shyness she had displayed on the initial meeting was fading away, replaced by a confidence that came from distain for a person. Viton almost faded into a daydream as she continued to rant. Still, this kind of backhand moaning was common amongst house staff, Viton needed more than a young maid's complaints if he was going to find out more about Samantha Highcliffe.

Stuffing clothing into the bag, Viton asked:

'Have you heard anything about the Lady disappearing? After I started, I heard some rumours she had run off somewhere once her parents had…' he paused, choosing his next words carefully, as he almost uttered that they had been murdered. '… Died,' he concluded.

Jessica smiled and twisted her long hair within her delicate fingers with a knowing look. 'This is only gossip mind, but I heard that she ran away to America. You know Lord Highcliffe?' Viton nodded, despite the answer being contrary. 'Well, he's no Lord, more of a buffoon really, we can all tell. The way he dresses, the way he speaks and the things he does – he can't be someone of high class.'

America, Viton thought, so that's where she disappeared, returning with 'Lord Highcliffe'. It was a start, but he'd have to find out something more concrete about that. Finishing placing the clothing into the bag, Jessica smiled sweetly.

'Thanks for the help. It was nice to moan to someone, everyone else is so stuck up, old fuddy duddys who are just happy to be in service.'

Viton could have left it there, but couldn't help but sarcastically remark.

'And you're different?'

She flinched, irked by the comment.

'I have dreams you know, I'm not going to be stuck here

forever, just you wait and see.' With that, and with an air of self-importance, she picked up the bags and strutted indoors and out of sight. Viton waited until she was gone before exiting the way he came in, slowly creeping down the hillside. Dreams, he laughed to himself, we all have them, until they are dragged through the hedge, stomped on and crushed by someone bigger and better off than us, then we are left to pick up the pieces. Removing the tie he had placed on to help him blend in, he buttoned his jacket as the air had turned cold. He decided to return to the office, to write up his notes and to do a bit of digging into this trip to America Samantha Highcliffe had taken. Navigating the crowd that were still perched at the bottom of the hill, he had almost escaped the rabble when he felt a firm grip on his arm tug him backward.

'Viton! I thought that was you skulking about,' Alfie Deron exclaimed, keeping a tight hold on Viton's arm so that he couldn't move. Despite his girth, he had a vice-like grip.

'Alfie.' Viton shot back bitterly.

'Let me guess, up to your old tricks? Just sneak up there to chat to the staff?' The problem with Alfie's re-emergence was that he knew all of Viton's tactics, after all, they had worked together for a length of time. Viton didn't want to give him the satisfaction of a reply, but his silence spoke volumes.

Alfie laughed. '*Ha!* I knew it! The vulture, picking out his prey again!' He smirked. 'Except this time, you're stuck in some dead-end town, at a worthless paper, *eh*?' Viton grimaced.

'Oh, yes, I've been asking around about you, my old mucker.' Alfie spat as he spoke. 'The people here, they don't like you. They also tell me the paper you write for is only good for one thing, wiping your ar—'

'All right!' Viton shouted, stopping Alfie's gloating. His grip loosened and Viton reclaimed his arm. Alfie had stopped smiling.

'Look, I'm only trying to help you,' Alfie said, although how gloating and mocking could be considered help, Viton wasn't sure. 'Get out of this town before the truth comes out. The people don't like you now. They certainly ain't gunna like you when they find out what happened before.'

Viton took a moment to consider his point before turning and storming off.

'Stay away from this one Viton!' Alfie called out. 'For your own good!' His protests faded into the wind as Viton headed back to the office, more determined than ever to expose Samantha Highcliffe.

***

By the time Viton left the office to meet with Lee, a thick layer of fog had rolled into the streets of Melford, making it impossible to see beyond a few meters in front of your face. The rich mist was cold, like tufts of ice hanging in the air, and Viton buried his head into his jacket as best he could. He'd spent some hours writing up his notes and informing

Madame Cherrie of his progress. She seemed to be happy to write any old gossip story, for she knew that given the current climate of the town it would sell. Viton wanted something grander but had to be careful, for as Alfie had warned, he did not want to expose his personal connection to Samantha Highcliffe just yet. The promise of a story that would change the way the town saw the good Lady was enough to seduce Cherrie though, and she had given him free rein to pursue the leads he had while she would write the puff piece about their arrival into the town. This suited Viton, as he could think of nothing worse than writing some guff, idolising the woman he despised.

Passing Brindles, Viton saw a small light, shining from within, reflecting on the frozen window panes. It could be Lee, but equally, it could be old man Brindle, hiding from that beast of a wife. Glancing at his watch, rubbing the condensation that glazed over it, he saw it was nearing eight p.m., the agreed time of their meeting. Not wishing to draw any unwanted attention by peering into the shop Viton scuttled by, suddenly becoming aware of a scuffling noise behind him, which had followed him the whole way from the office. Every time he glanced back, however, he was met with only the shadows of the buildings, the gleam of the cobbles of the street and that thick, elusive fog.

Deciding it was nothing to fear, Viton slipped into the alleyway. Somehow the fog was even more focused down here, making each step a calculated risk. Leaning against the wall, Viton waited, inspecting what little he could of the alleyway. Beside him, a pool of water, as dark as night. Small ripples shook through the water as he stood, as if something or someone were moving nearby. Glancing back at the alleyway entrance, Viton saw no one though. It was at this moment that Lee emerged, holding a small lantern in hand. Clearly, it had been him that he had spied in Brindles shop.

'Mr V-V-Viton?' Lee stammered out, holding the lantern close to his face, its gleam reflecting in his spectacles. Viton moved closer.

'Keep your voice down,' Viton whispered in a hushed tone.

'S-Sorry sir,' Lee said, more quietly this time. Viton could see from his face that the young man was anxious, as the lantern shook from the trembling of his hand.

'Well?' Viton asked, eager to escape the alleyway. Lee looked around nervously, before reaching into his pocket and retrieving a bundle of crumpled letters, tied loosely with string.

'Did you get everything I wanted?' Viton pressed, snatching the letters from Lee and placing them into his own jacket.

'It's all there,' Lee replied, afraid, 'the letters from the owner of Ashbrook, the letters from the Highcliffe's, everything.'

'Good,' Viton said, smiling sadistically as the lantern cast a golden glow across his sinister face.

'I'll need them back sir,' Lee said timidly.

'Need them back?' Viton raised his voice slightly as Lee

backed away.

'Mr Brindle, he'll know they've been taken! When he realises…' Lee trailed off.

Viton sighed. 'The old bat won't notice anything, you've seen the mountain of paperwork. Just claim it's amongst them and leave him to search through it. I'll give you them back as soon as the stories written.' Lee's face lit up at this.

'Thank you, sir, thank you,' he repeated as if a huge burden had been removed from his shoulders. Viton knew he wouldn't be thanking him by the time the story was published, both he and Mr Brindle were likely to lose the largest client they'd ever had if he had his way. Feeling a pang of guilt for both this realisation and his actions the previous day, Viton reached into his pocket and produced a roll of notes.

'Here. Take this.' He held out the money outstretched as Lee looked at it perplexed. 'For your trouble.' Viton thrust the money more forcefully toward him.

Lee was gazing down at the money, only dimly illuminated by the lantern, when there was a sudden crash behind them, causing Lee and Viton to jump. Spinning around, they saw a shadow lingering in the entranceway, cursing loudly. In a flash, Viton ran forward, dropping the money in front of Lee, who after scooping it up, followed after. The figure turned to flee but before he got far, Viton tackled him to the ground, and they landed painfully upon the bumpy cobbles. Adrenaline coursing through his veins, Viton dove on top of the figure, pinning him to the ground as Lee arrived holding the lantern. The light revealed the squinting face of Alfie Deron.

'*Argh*... my back...' Alfie writhed in pain. Lee looked on concerned and went to reach out a hand, but Viton shook his head furiously, causing him to back away.

'What are you doing here Alfie? Why were you watching us?' Viton hissed.

Alfie grimaced as he spoke, 'Knew you'd have a lead...' he gasped for breath, Viton's grip unwavering, '... after I saw you this morning. Waited at your office... followed you when you left...' he coughed and spluttered, '... saw you bribing this kid...'

Lee was horrified. 'He was not bribing me!'

Alfie spat onto the ground next to him before saying, 'He was just handing you a role of notes as a friend then, was he?'

Lee looked ashamed and turned away, while Viton's blood began to boil.

'You told me to stay away from this!' he exclaimed. 'You just want the glory for yourself!'

Alfie stared deep into Viton's eyes as he yelled, 'You're damn right, I do! This story could make my career! You... you're washed up, it's too late for you, but me...' Alfie trailed off.

Viton felt a rage – a feral, animalistic rage, deep within him, one that had never been tapped into before. He drew back his hand and clenching into a tight fist, struck Alfie clean across the face, blood spurting from the man's nose like a fountain. Without thinking, he readied himself for another blow, but as he raised his arm, he was held back by Lee, who dropped the lantern, which smashed and extinguished on the cold, hard floor.

'Stop, sir! Stop!' Lee cried desperately. 'Don't do something you'll regret,' he pleaded.

Engulfed by the dark and the fog, Viton could only make out the outline of Alfie, who was cradling his bloodied nose, moaning meekly, as it leaked onto the cobbled streets. Viton still had a fist clenched, his arm pulsating, part of him longed to deliver another blow to Alfie. Yet the voice of Lee, the desperation and fear, brought him to his senses and he slowly lowered his arm. Leaning in close to Alfie, still pinning him to the ground, Viton whispered into his ear:

'This is my story. It began with me, it ends with me. You don't get to steal it. Not you. Not anyone. She's mine. Leave. Don't come back. If you do, I'll find you.'

He released his grip and rose up, standing beside Lee. The pair watched as Alfie dragged himself off the floor, holding his nose and without saying a word he shuffled off into the fog, disappearing.

'What did you say to him?' Lee asked innocently.

Viton shook his head. 'Don't worry about it.'

Lee reached into his pocket and retrieved the bundle of notes.

'This is yours,' he offered it back to Viton. Waving a hand, Viton said:

'Please, just take it.' Lee thrust the money into Viton's bloodied hands.

'No,' Lee said plainly. He turned to leave but lingered there in the street for a moment.

'Something you want to ask?' Viton asked.

Lee froze, seemingly uncertain of his next course of action. After a moment had passed, he seemed to find the courage somewhere to ask:

'Well. When we met, sir, that night at the pub? You seemed... I don't know... lonely? But kind. Something about you was kind. Mr Brindle and the others, they treated you with malice but you didn't raise a hand in violence... you could have flattened an old man like Mr Brindle,' he delivered the speech with regular, anxious pauses.

'Your point?' Viton asked coldly.

'My point is... well... What changed?'

The question seemed to linger in the air, like the fog, the answer, elusive, even to Viton. Finding himself unable to form an answer, Viton stuffed the notes, now bloodied from being in his hands, into his pocket and, after checking the letters were still in his jacket, wandered into the dark, foggy night. After a few moments, he was lost from view.

VII

For a couple of days, Samantha busied herself with the comings and goings of the furniture, ordering and arranging their positions within the new house. The events of the first night were largely forgotten, lost in a whirlwind of household objects and people frantically asking for her approval on almost everything. The one stark reminder was the cuts, still sore, on her hands. However, she had come to find that she could no longer tolerate her husband's constant intrusions, for he would come wandering, pocking his nose into her business and generally acting as a nuisance. Perhaps she felt this way as she was coming to the dawning realisation of how much money he had squandered on tasteless art depicting crude images of violence and nudity. Samantha had no doubt that Randell saw these pieces as a symbol of his newfound rank and class, for he admired them all greatly. Really, they just showed how base he was. As one of the pieces was carried by, Randell rushed over and ripped it from the hands of the staff holding it, taking some time to stare at it intensely. Samantha shoed the two servants away, as they had been lingering, uncertain of if they should retrieve the piece from their master. Looking over her husband's shoulder, Samantha saw the painting delineate a gladiator locked in a gruesome battle with a lion. The image was not well formed nor particularly tasteful, yet Randell insisted it be given pride of place in the drawing room above the fireplace. Hanging it there, he took a few steps back to admire it, allowing his hands to rest on his hips as he gazed proudly. Samantha was sure that Randell saw himself amongst the painting, remembering that fateful night she had met him, when he had protected her. Sure enough, he confirmed this by turning to her and muttering:

'I'm just like this gladiator, your faithful protector, remember?' His tone was nostalgic, and she too could not resist feeling so, thinking back to those happy, simpler times. When she had met Randell, she was not Samantha Highcliffe, heir to the Highcliffe fortune and estate, she was simply herself. Perhaps that is why she had fled in the first place, she had wanted to find herself out there, anywhere that was not her dreaded family estate. She had managed to be free of her family's long shadows for a time, but now seemed to find herself in a new prison of her own making. The memories of Randell and her family brought swelling tears to her eyes, not of sadness, but of pity for herself and her position. Samantha wanted to escape the Manor and with Randell still entranced by his garish painting, she slunk off down a hallway, rushing past a serving girl who inquired half-heartedly as to if her lady was all right. Undeterred, Samantha soldiered on by, not stopping for anyone or anything, and she soon found herself outside, the fresh breeze of the outdoors cooling her somewhat.

Leaving the giggles and whispers of gossiping staff behind, Samantha found joy in the outdoors, heading for the small garden at the side of the Manor, which had become her own private sanctuary. She walked with purpose, wanting to escape any prying eyes, and shuffled into the closed-off area, hidden by a row of towering bushes. Some would have called it a sad sight, as much like the overgrowth which clung to the house walls, the garden was like a weed-filled jungle. Samantha found solace here though, a place where she could hide away, lost amongst the winding vines and plants. Her favourite spot was a slightly rusted metal bench, Samantha imagined it as a relic of a past owner and could almost picture previous residents sitting on a sunny day, enjoying the majesty of the garden patch. Perching herself upon it, Samantha examined the surroundings in an attempt to calm her mind.

The area was laid out in a spherical formation, a small concrete slabbed path leading around, with the hedges obscuring vision from the outside as they lined the edges of the path. Once, she thought, they may have been fashioned into all manner of decorative and artistic shapes, yet now they stood, almost sombrely, as if they had been alive far too long. Indeed, it was as if the entire garden had been alive too long, or far too long for anyone to care any more. Samantha imagined the plants, vengeful at being forgotten, reclaiming the land as its own, which they had succeeded in. Wild overgrowths protruded from beneath the man-made concrete, cracking and rupturing the slabs.

The wild garden contrasted in almost every way with the Highcliffe estate garden, where she had spent much of her youth. She recalled many afternoons spent wallowing the time away, smelling the roses in full bloom, tending to the new flowers with her mother, helping the servants to harvest crops, or climbing their apple trees in search of a juicy snack. While these were happy hazy memories, they were now tinged with an air of sadness, as with time she had come to realise that the garden was nothing more than a holding cell for her. The most vivid memory of her time in the garden was when, one summer's day, she was sat in the apple tree and noticed that a branch, one that had been overlooked while being trimmed, had grown longer and was now like an outstretched arm reaching over the walls that surrounded the Highcliffe estate. Samantha had never left the estate, her parents (particularly her father), warned her constantly of the dangers of the outside, the clawing vultures of the paupers who would steal all they held dear. However, Samantha was a clever child and adept at hiding and listening. She came to know a new enemy, the dreaded press, which her father ranted, raved and loathed with all of his heart. One time, while hidden away in a small cupboard, she heard her father prostrating that the press had the power to build you up to the highest heights and push you off the pedestal they had built before clawing at your corpse once it had hit the ground. Despite the constant reinforcement not to go into the outside world, a mix of simple human psychology and a child's curiosity got the better of Samantha that day, when she saw the branch which could lead her outside into a world that was new, dangerous and exciting.

Without thinking, as if compelled by an unseen force, she began to shuffle along the branch, unseen by her mother and the servants below, due to the thick leaves growing upon the tree. It was only as she emerged at the end of the branch that she was spotted, but despite the heckles of those around her, she would not be stopped, not now that the new world was so close. Jumping forward, she propelled herself over the estate walls and landed on the fresh grass outside. While behind her chaos had erupted, the noise from behind faded away, becoming little more than a distant buzzing as she drank in the sight of the vast expanses. She had seen the fields and town from her window before, but had never felt what it was like until now. She knelt down in the grass and ripped a handful of it from the ground feeling it within her palm. Something about this felt different, even the air itself felt different, she felt a feeling rising within her that she had never experienced before, a sense of awe, wonder and a longing to see more. The escape was short lived however, as the staff had quickly mobilised and found her, marching her back into the estate, the gates slamming shut with a clink, the locks turning with a sense of finality. She was led to her father, who savagely berated her, yelling hysterically about the dangers of the outside and if she had been seen. Sentenced to her room, she heard her poor mother bearing the brunt of the anger and Samantha was haunted by the sight of the bruises inflicted by her father. From that moment on, she never attempted to leave again.

Now, back in the present, she lamented being stuck in another prison, for fear of being hounded by the ravenous press. If her father had been right about one thing, it was their ability to destroy a person, regardless of their stature. That is why she was frustrated by but also feared Randell's cocksure attitude, his blatant disregard for hiding the truth. He would often bound around the home, reminiscing loudly about his previous position and while the staff no doubt nattered amongst themselves, so far, their large pay slips had kept mouths silent. Samantha knew the truth was bound to come out eventually and could prove their undoing, if they were not careful. Perhaps this is why she enjoyed the overgrown garden. Here she could sit, hidden, still, quietly away from the eyes of others. She did not have to be Samantha Highcliffe, she could be alone with her thoughts and unafraid of what lurked just outside.

Suddenly her attention was drawn by the sound of horses and carriages around by the front of the house. Rushing from the garden recluse, Samantha rounded the corner to the front of the house in time to see Randell being ferried away by a carriage down the path into the town. Heading over to where a serving girl stood, Samantha said:

'Where is my husband going?' Allowing some of the trepidation in her voice to slip through.

'He said he wanted to go out into the town, ma'am,' the young girl replied harmlessly enough, before adding: 'I think he wanted to get a feel for the local theatres.'

Samantha scoffed. She had expressly forbidden him from drawing any unnecessary attention to them and had pleaded that he stay home for the first week of their residence at the Manor so that the press would not look into their business. She could already picture the crowds and leeches questioning him as he disembarked in the town, a thought which filled her with anger and dread.

'Are you all right, ma'am? You've gone quite ashen-faced,' the girl replied, concernedly. Samantha touched her face with her palm, the cuts still fresh from the other night. Her skin was icy to touch.

'I'm fine, I'm fine,' Samantha insisted before she turned and fled, her mind racing with the endless ways in which Randell would cause her downfall. Heading back toward the garden, lost in her own world, she didn't notice the overgrown vines on the side of the house, warping and twisting, digging deeper into the building.

VIII

Sipping on the bitter liquid, Viton grimaced as it touched his lips. For the last few days he had been slaving away at his desk, under strict instruction from Madame Cherrie. Having examined the letters shortly after obtaining them, Viton had been underwhelmed by what he had found. The letters from the Highcliffe's were largely written by Lord Highcliffe, who came across as little more than a bumbling oaf, and little was said of their rumoured life in America. Samantha Highcliffe was almost entirely absent from the letters, which aided Viton very little in his quest. He placed the coffee cup down and picked up the telephone receiver.

From across the room Madame Cherrie sat at her desk. Unfortunately, Madame Cherrie had found something that piqued her interest amongst the letters, and that was the name of the elusive owners of Ashbrook Manor. At first Cherrie had seemed apprehensive as to where Viton had retrieved the letters from, but upon learning that the owner of Ashbrook Manor was named in one of the crumpled parchments, all anxieties had left her. She had snatched the letter from him, pouring over every word and detail for quite some time.

Viton shook his head dismissively, for the owners of the old house didn't really bother him. He was in the middle of calling an old acquaintance, Squeaky Eddie, from his previous paper in an attempt to find out what he knew about the Highcliffes. He got the name Squeaky Eddie as he always made sure his sources were squeaky clean before printing anything. He called it rigour, the others saw it as a pointless waste of time, but he did always have reliable information. Viton had found him harmless enough and hoped that he would be willing to share any information he had. They had just got through the pleasantries, the how are you's, long time no speak, etc. and Viton was rapidly losing interest in Eddie's monotone droll and was keen to press on.

'Listen Eddie, while I've got you on the phone, I don't suppose you remember anything about what happened with that Highcliffe case a couple of years back? Did you ever catch any wind of where she ended up after all the rumours came out?'

There was a long silent pause from the other end of the line.

'Don't tell me you're in Melford, Viton?' Eddie said, suspiciously, 'you know that report brought you bad luck... you should just leave it alone.'

Viton sighed, knowing Eddie's character, he found honesty was the best policy, as he could close up if he suspected a person of lying, 'Eddie, I'll be straight with you, I am in Melford. I work for the local paper here now and I'm sure you know the Highcliffes have just moved into the old Manor here.'

Viton imagined Eddie rubbing his forehead on the other end of the line, something he had always done whenever he was slightly stressed or inconvenienced. Eddie's silence continued, but he hadn't hung up yet, so Viton pushed on hopefully.

'We're working on a story about the Highcliffe family here, writing a bit about them so the locals can get a feel for them. Can you shed a bit of light on where Samantha went after that whole incident?'

Eddie was quiet for a while before saying:

'I heard what happened with Alfie.'

The statement lingered, echoed, and vibrated down the line as if Viton was hearing it over and over. His hands, still red from the force with which he had struck him, began to shake slightly. Eddie sighed loudly.

'You're lucky that I never liked the guy Viton. Seeing as you did what I never could, I'll tell you a bit of what I know.'

Viton smiled and thanked Eddie.

'I'm not being used as a source, okay? This is strictly information, nothing to be quoted, all right?'

Viton agreed, after all he never planned on using Eddie as a source, but information was power in this game and the more he could get the better.

'We've got a source come in that claims to have known both Lord and Lady Highcliffe when they both lived in America.' Viton nodded as he scrambled to find a notepad and pen. Madame Cherrie was still pondering the letter about the Manor, but passed over her ballpoint pen as Viton looked for one. The rumour about the life in America had been true, he was pleased to find out.

'This is where it gets interesting, you won't believe this part. The source claims that she used to be part of a circus act. She was a juggler, with her twin. One night they're performing in a small town and the ringleader defends a girl from a tiger. Next thing they know, the girl is travelling with them day in day out, she's enamoured with their charismatic leader. Sadly, it all came crashing down when their big top was set on fire by hooligans. Well there was only a few performers and they had little money, so the group disbanded. This juggler claims that the girl was Samantha Highcliffe and her new husband, the ringleader. Dressed up in pompous clothing and trying to pass himself off as a member of high-society.'

Viton had stopped scribbling on his notepad, it almost seemed too farfetched to be true.

'Why has this source come forward now then? If she knew her a year or so ago?'

Eddie's droll had been replaced with a genuinely excitable tone. 'Well, the pieces everyone's been writing in the papers about the move, someone got a hold of the information from somewhere and pictures of the pair have been circulating. The girl claims that she recognises both of them. I'm looking into the truth of the matter, but this travelling circus weren't registered anywhere. At the moment all we've got is her word.'

Viton was sceptical of the whole story, but then it was so bizarre, who in their right mind could have made it up?

'Will you let me know if you find out the truth? It all sounds a bit like this source is trying to get some attention for herself to me.'

Eddie said he would, before continuing, 'Viton, you said you're in Melford right?'

Viton cautiously said, 'Yeah, I am. Why?'

'The paper here, to go along with all this Highcliffe story we've been looking into Ashbrook Manor. To tell you the truth it's a bit of an anomaly, we can't really find any information on it at all. By all physical accounts, it just appeared one day. Do you know anything about it?'

Viton looked over at Madame Cherrie, who was now reclining in her chair, engrossed by the bundle of letters. Turning away and keeping his voice low, he said:

'I've got some info here yeah. But what's in it for me?'

Eddie chuckled at the other end of the line, so loudly that he was worried it might draw the attention of Cherrie.

'Still the same old vulture, looking for your cut. Listen, I like you Viton, what happened to you wasn't right. I think enough time has passed, if you can give us something concrete, a story, details on that house, I think there's a good chance I could get you back in the fold.' He paused for a moment. 'Would you be interested in that?'

Viton glanced over his desk at Cherrie, who signalled for him to wrap up his call. Unsure of what to say, Eddie replied:

'I'll take your silence as a yes, of course you want to get out of that little town and back to the big leagues. Get back to me when you have something, then send it over to me. I'll let you know about the Highcliffe situation in the meantime.

IX

Samantha clung tightly to the bedcovers as a fierce wind howled like a pack of wolves outside. It seemed as if the house itself was shaking with the force of the gale and Samantha feared that she would get little rest. Besides the wind, her mind was flooded with rampaging thoughts, as some hours earlier Randell had returned home and announced his grand idea of holding a party. Samantha had been, expectedly, furious at the very suggestion, which was why Randell had already placed the advertisement into the paper before returning, so she had no choice but to supersede to his plans. Enraged at his trickery, she had ordered the staff to make up the second bedroom immediately, as she was to sleep separately from her husband that night. Randell tried to protest, but knew that it was best to let her stupor for a while.

Thus, she laid, alone in the spare bedroom, which was meagerly decorated. Every time she turned to attempt to find a comfy spot, the bed would creak eerily and in the dark of night with only the howling winds as companion, she could not help but recall the first night on which they had arrived. In her head she imagined the ominous chiming and had a vague recollection of shadowy figures over a bed, but the memory was hazy, as was often the case with half-remembered dreams. She had convinced herself that it was a dream, for that was the only way she could explain the strange occurrence and the only way she could justify sleeping in the house. The cuts on her hand remained though, a painful reminder that she could not ignore, no matter how much she tried to reason with herself.

She tossed and turned for what felt like hours in the darkness as she attempted to find comfort and peace of mind. It was then, in the very dead of night, that she heard the handle of the bedroom door begin to twist, a low grating metal crunching emanating from it as it did so. Sitting upright and holding the covers close, Samantha hissed in the general direction of the door:

'If that is you Randell, don't even bother.' She imagined him on the other side, plotting to use his passionate ways to woo her, he wanting to play the part of hero on a menacing night such as this. Yet, despite her warning, the door handle continued to twist until Samantha heard the doorframe open gently.

'Randell, I'm warning you.' Samantha projected once again into the dark. Something about this didn't seem right to her, and she felt a chill slowly slither down her spine. It was unlike him to stay silent so long. That was when she heard the sounds of timid footsteps coming into the room. As her eyes adjusted to the darkness, she could make out a figure in the doorway, lingering like a spectre.

'Who's there?' Samantha asked, her voice trembling as she spoke. It was as if the figure tilted their head at her before moving toward the bed. It was as if she were gliding, almost silently, over the floor and Samantha recoiled as far back as she could as the figure continued its ominous approach.

A low, gentle voice rang out as the figure stopped at the end of the bed.

'Come to me dear...' the voice was soft and bizarrely comforted Samantha, despite the situation. 'Come to your mother...' the voice continued. Yet Samantha knew her mother's voice, and this was not it.

'Can I help you?' Samantha asked, trembling under the covers. Reaching to her bedside, she instinctively went to light the lantern placed there by the servants. The figure lingered, now unspeaking and waited until the amber light was shining, giving Samantha a clearer view of the thing before her. Samantha was confronted by the visage of an aging withered woman, more bone than flesh. She looked underfed and malnourished, with pale white skin. Oddly, she wore a tattered maid's uniform, the likes of which Samantha had not seen for many years. Without speaking, the figure crept onto the end of the bed, making weightless indents into the covers, her form becoming clearer by the moment. She moved, weakly, toward Samantha. Her face was strewn with wrinkles, her hair greying and frayed with clumps missing, revealing a raw, aged scalp. Samantha was like a statue, unable to move or take her eyes off of the approaching spectre. Outside, the wind had suddenly stilled and the room fell deathly silent as the woman came to rest just in front of Samantha. She opened her skeletal arms, as if waiting for an embrace. Samantha sat unmoving, unable to even speak as the figure waited for what felt like hours. Then she reached out and tugged Samantha's hands from under the covers, pressing on the cuts upon her hands. She would have winced in pain, but she found she couldn't even make a sound.

After a moment, the woman let go of Samantha's hands, returning them to her. Looking down at them, Samantha saw they were dripping with blood. She looked up in terror at the woman, whose face was now also covered with splatters of rose red blood. Still, the woman smiled, revealing a row of rotten teeth and tentatively placed a bony finger over Samantha's lips.

'*Hush* now...' she whispered softly, '... Mother's here...' Samantha closed her eyes tightly, fearful of what the spectre wanted. Suddenly the room was engulfed in a blinding white light emanating from the window, followed by a deafening rumbling of thunder.

Samantha jumped and opened her eyes, seeing before her the two shadowy figures at her bedside. The old woman was gone, vanished as if a ghost, but these new figures were something else, something inhuman. Her mind raced as memories of the first night's encounter filled her head, these were the same beasts as she had seen before. They were unmoving, yet their bodies continually twisted and contorted in the darkness, it was impossible to tell where they began and ended. All that could be seen was the harrowing glow of a pair of white lights, as if eyes that hung above her bed. It felt as if the very house itself was spinning, twirling and whirling all around her. Gripping the bed tightly, she felt as if she were going to be sick as she cried out as loudly as she could for Randell. Over and over she yelled, but it was as if, despite her throat feeling raw, no sound was produced.

Without warning, the bedroom door creaked open and just as quickly as the figures had appeared, they vanished, leaving nothing but the darkness of an empty room. Gasping, trying to catch her breath, Samantha heard Randell call out:

'My dear, are you all right? I could hear you thumping about from the other side of the landing.'

Samantha tried to speak but couldn't, instead producing rasping sounds as if she were unable to breathe. Randell rushed to her bedside and held her as she grabbed at him. By now, the servants had been awoken by the commotion and were congregating by the bedroom door.

'My dear, are you all right?' Randell asked, feeling her skin. It was icy cold to the touch and she had become frighteningly pale. 'Get her some whiskey and phone a doctor at once!' Randell barked at the servants, who were stood around helplessly, watching the spectacle unfold. Randell embraced his wife, holding her close and trying to warm her frozen skin. Soon, Jessica, the serving maid, appeared holding a small beaker of whiskey, which Randell poured down Samantha's throat forcefully. The liquid burned as it travelled through her body, but allowed her to catch her breath enough to speak.

'Oh Randell…' she cried out, tears of fear rolling down her cheeks. 'It was awful… I saw the most terrible things…'

Randell placed a finger to her lips, silencing her.

'Don't talk now dear. We have a doctor on the way, try to conserve your strength.' He lay her down gently in her bed, propping her up with pillows. From downstairs, there was a booming knock on the front door. Instructing Jessica to remain by her bedside, Randell rushed downstairs to allow the doctor entry to the Manor. Jessica knelt down beside the bed and tentatively held her Lady's limp hand.

Samantha remembered little of the next set of events, only recovering her full senses sometime later. She was still in the bed, the covers wrapped tightly around her. She wanted to move, yet as she did so she found all of her muscles ached unbearably and her head was spinning. Resigning to laying in the bed, she could hear the doctor and Randell speaking outside of the bedroom door.

'Are you saying my wife is hysterical?' Randell barked.

'No Lord Highcliffe, what I am saying is she has obviously been under a lot of stress recently and this can lead to certain... outcomes,' the doctor said politely.

'What can be done about it?' Randell retorted angrily.

The doctor coughed slightly before replying, 'I would suggest bedrest and lots of it. Good hearty food and plenty of drink. She is not to do anything strenuous for at least a week. I will come back and see her, then we can make our assessment.'

Samantha heard Randell pace across the landing before hissing.

'We're supposed to be hosting a party in two days for

the whole town. Will she be all right for that?'

The doctor scoffed, 'Good heavens no, sir. She must rest, it is imperative for her health, both physically and...' He trailed off.

It was Randell's turn to scoff now. 'Yes, yes, I get the picture.' He paused for a moment. 'Thank you doctor. Come, I'd better see you out.'

Their voices and footsteps faded away as they left the landing and Samantha was left in the silence of the bedroom. With all her might she turned her head to face the window. The storm was still raging, the occasional flash of lightning hurting her eyes, the roar of the thunder shaking her to the core. She barely had the strength to even consider what had happened to her, but, despite her exhaustion, she did not sleep, for she felt, out there in the stormy night, a dark presence was still watching her.

X

The morning air was cool and the street still damp as Viton watched Brindles from across the street. Having spent the previous afternoon trawling through documents in the dingey, dusty basement of the public records building he didn't mind standing out in the fresh air, in fact, he drank it in more deeply because of this.

After being tasked with finding out more about Mr Brindles supposed ownership of Ashbrook Manor, Viton knew he was going to need facts to present to the man, as the memory of his previous conversation at the pub hung within his mind. Thus, he had headed over to the public records building. Quite frankly, it wasn't much to look at, a small, bland box-shaped building housed more bland box-shaped rooms, all an off-white colour, as if dulled and aged. When he asked the receptionist about documentation for Ashbrook Manor, she spent a great deal of time shifting through the filing system behind her. It didn't help that she looked as if she were as old as the building itself, and Viton was sure her eyesight was failing her, as she opened the same cabinet in search of the documents three times in a row. Finally, after much searching, she emerged with some paperwork, smiling sweetly at Viton as she handed it over. He shot a wry, sarcastic smile back as he navigated the stairs down to the basement area to study the papers.

Clearing space on a desk, he laid out the paperwork before him. A thick cloud of dust spewed across the room like fog, as the papers clearly hadn't been touched in some time. The first piece of documentation that caught Viton's eye was architectural sketches of the house, which showed views inside and outside of the Manor. The drawings depicted a large dining hall and drawing room in the lower section of the house, while the upstairs floor plan showed at least eight bedrooms. Why would a Manor need so many bedrooms? Viton couldn't help but wonder. The exterior design looked largely like what he had seen up close, but still his curiosity for visiting the Manor had been peaked, and he knew that in two days' time he would get his chance when he attended the Highcliffe's party.

The architectural drawings only showed so much though and had very little value to Viton's investigation as he could not find reference as to when the designs were drawn up or which company was contracted to build the structure. Studying the other paperwork, he stumbled upon a copy of the land deed, which, just as the letter from the office had indicated, had Brindles name on it. He had purchased the land forty years prior, there was no disputing that, so in essence Ashbrook Manor was his. Viton was curious though, how could a man of meagre means like Mr Brindle finance the construction of a lavish Manor house? He knew that Brindle had extortionate rates at his agency, but even then, he would struggle to pay for a structure like the Manor.

More bizarrely than this though, was a list of residents – people who had resided at the structure built on Brindle's land. There must have been more than two dozen names, mainly families, groups of wives, husbands and children. This in itself wasn't odd, but none of these groups had acquired tenancy for longer than a month each. Some of the families had even arrived in the last year, when Viton himself was in Melford, yet he could not recall ever meeting or hearing of them. For as long as he, and it seemed everyone else in the town, had known Ashbrook Manor had been empty. He studied the list carefully, finding the most recent tenants, prior to the Highcliffe's, a family by the name of the Smiths. Viton wracked his brain, really thinking deeply for a moment, and in his mind, he could see the silhouettes of a family of four – a wife, husband, two young children – but they were shadowy and unclear. When he attempted to look closer, it was like staring at a photo that had faded over time, their features became blurry streaks and the image was painful to hang onto. Viton rubbed his temple, allowing the memory to vanish. What had happened to this family and why couldn't he remember them? For that matter, what had happened to all of the previous tenants? Something was wrong, Viton knew it. Brindle had a lot to answer.

Now, stood across the street from Brindles, Viton took out the list of previous tenants, which he had managed to steal from the public records building, as the old dear at reception had not even checked the documents he had returned, and studied them closely, readying himself to confront Brindle. Viton had never thought much of him, but he was unassuming in a way, he went about his life in a callous, grumpy manner, but that was just how he was, the people of Melford seemed to have all come to a consensus on that. Could he really be involved in some kind of sinister plot? Viton had his doubts, he was almost certain it was some kind of scam, he just hadn't figured out how it worked yet. Looking back up at the agency, he spotted Lee opening the door with his keys. Viton was sure that Brindle would have been there earlier than his young companion, so decided to head over and find out where the old man was.

Ding! A small bell chimed as Viton entered the shop.

'Good morning, just wait a moment and I'll be right wit-' Lee had been hanging his jacket on a coatrack in the corner as Viton entered, but mid-speech had turned around. 'Ah, it's you,' he said, unsurely. 'What do you want?' he spoke warily, Viton imagined he was worried that his theft of the letters might be unearthed.

Viton took a seat casually in front of Lee and with his thumb gestured toward Brindle's office.

'Boss not in yet?'

Lee looked over at the office and then met eyes with Viton before quickly glancing nervously away.

'What do you want with him?' Lee's voice wavered slightly as he spoke. He still hadn't taken a seat at his desk, he remained frozen awkwardly behind it. Viton folded his arms.

'When will he be back? I've got some questions for him.'

Lee rubbed his hands together anxiously.

'He called me last night and said he's away on business for a few days, I've got to mind the agency for a while.' Lee looked over at Viton, who was thinking deeply. 'I'm telling you the truth,' he protested.

'I know you are,' Viton said, standing up and heading over to the office door.

'It'll be locked, sir!' Lee called out, still not moving from his desk.

Viton tried to turn the knob but found it was stiff. Locked, just as Lee had said. Viton resumed his seat and stroked his chin, thinking. This all seemed too convenient. Just as he and Cherrie found out about his ownership of Ashbrook and these disappearances, Brindle leaves town? Was it just a coincidence or was there more to this?

'Please, sir, if you've got nothing else to do here...' Lee perked up, clearly desperate to be out of his presence. Viton reached into his pocket and dug out the letter proclaiming Brindle as the owner of Ashbrook. He tossed it onto the desk in front of Lee.

'Read that,' he said commandingly.

Lee picked up the crumpled letter and began to read, the parchment shaking slightly as his hands trembled. After a few moments, the shaking stopped and Lee placed down the letter, a look of bewilderment on his face.

'So you didn't know either.' Viton sighed, he had hoped

Lee might be able to shed some light on the situation.

'Mr Brindle owns Ashbrook? But...' Lee trailed off, deeply confused.

'It's true,' Viton explained, 'went down to the public records to check for myself. He owns the land Ashbrook is built on.'

Lee was staring at the letter, deep in thought.

'You had no idea about this? Despite the fact you work with him?' Viton pressed, leaning forward onto the edge of Lee's desk. Lee bolted upright, defensively stating:

'Sir, this is as much a shock to you as it is to me. I had no idea. I went up and valued the place and he said nothing, he's like that you see. He doesn't always give me all the details about clients, he mostly handles that, I just do the valuing and generally show the people around the houses and such.'

Viton reclined slightly, he figured Lee was telling the truth, as he was still clearly afraid of him. He felt a pang of guilt, for in truth the lad was a nice enough chap, but at least it meant he was speaking earnestly.

'Did Brindle say why he'd gone out of town?' Viton pondered.

Lee shook his head. 'He just said business, but that's his way, he sometimes goes off for a while. He never gives me the full details and I've learnt not to ask.'

The two sat in silence for a moment, both thinking deeply about the mystery of the Manor. Lee broke the silence, talking more to himself than to Viton.

'To think Mr Brindle owns that huge Manor... why does he bother with all this agency business? He clearly has a small fortune somewhere!'

Viton reached into his pocket and produced the document with the list of names, presenting it to Lee.

'Do you recognize any of these names?'

Lee skimmed the document quickly before shaking his head.

'I don't think so...'

Viton stared at him. 'These are people who've lived up on that land where Ashbrook is. Look at the dates.' He pointed at the dates so Lee could clearly see them.

Lee looked at them, whispering under his breath, 'They've only lived there a month each...'

Viton leant in close again. 'You say you show the families around, you must have shown them to Ashbrook Manor, or whatever was there before.'

Lee locked eyes with Viton, this time unflinchingly.

'I'm telling you, sir, the first time I've been up to the Manor to value it was before the Highcliffe's moved in, I've never gone there before and I don't know who these people are.'

His defiance was enough to convince Viton he was telling the truth, or at least believed he was. He was about to retrieve the document from the table when Lee placed his hand on it, looking closely once again.

'Wait a minute... the Rivers family... I think I...' Lee trailed off, as if lost in a daydream. Suddenly, he winced and held his head in his hands.

'Are you all right?' Viton leant forward, caringly placing a hand on Lee's shoulder. Recoiling at the touch, Lee shook it off.

'I'm fine... I'm fine...' He repeated. Viton retrieved the document and stuffed it back into his pocket.

'Did you say you remembered the Rivers family?' Viton asked curiously. Lee looked at him for a moment, as if saddened by the thought before shaking his head and simply saying:

'No, I was wrong.'

Viton nodded, not wishing to pry any further. He stood up as if to leave before asking.

'When is Brindle due back?'

Lee had recovered his senses slightly and said:

'He'll be back in two days.'

Viton was pleased, he could catch him after the Highcliffe party. Turning to leave, Lee suddenly asked:

'Sir... Where are the other letters I gave you?' Viton turned back and saw the face of Lee, like a child afraid of being scolded, waiting for his answer. He weighed up telling him the truth, that Lord Highcliffe had retrieved the letters and would no doubt be complaining to Brindle as soon as he was able, but figured he had caused the chap enough pain over the last few days.

'They're back at the office,' Viton said dismissively, turning to face away from Lee. 'I'll get them back to you as soon as I'm done with the story.'

In the reflection of the windows, Viton saw Lee breathe a sigh of relief. 'Thank you, sir,' he said, putting the letter about the ownership of Ashbrook into his desk. Viton nodded and promptly left the agency, the bell chiming once again as he headed out onto the streets. He paused once he had crossed the street and took a moment to think. It seemed his investigation of the Manor was on hold. With the Highcliffe party only a day away, he was free to focus on finding out more about the dreaded Samantha Highcliffe and ready himself to come face-to-face with her.

As he stood, thinking, he felt an uneasy feeling in the pit of his stomach. Like a mouse, spied from afar by a predatory owl, he felt he was being watched by someone. Above Brindles, the looming figure of Mrs Brindle stood, leering at him through the window, unseen by Viton. Her eyes were sharpened, beady and penetrating.

XI

The last two days had been painful for Samantha. Despite being bedridden and exhausted, she did not allow herself to sleep for fear of what might find her in the night. This irrational fear lingered but went unaccepted as she had quickly learnt that any attempt to explain her visions was met with dismissal, especially on the part of Randell, who was still persevering with his preparations for the party, insisting that Samantha would be well enough to attend by the time evening fell.

Her day consisted of laying, longingly staring out of the window, a view of her garden just below. How she longed to walk in the fresh air, amongst those wild weeds, but alas, she did not have the strength to do so. She was waited on hand and foot by servants, they delivered food to her and changed bedpans. They inwardly loathed her, as Samantha inwardly loathed them, for she was sure that as soon as they returned to their servants' quarters they would revel in gossiping about her, complaining to one another about each and every little flaw their lady possessed.

On one such visit, the youngest maid, Jessica, arrived, cradling a box full of journals.

'My lady?' she said tentatively as she entered the room.

She could see that Samantha was gazing outside, her eyes glazed over as if she were a million miles away. Tiptoeing closer, she called out to her again. This time it caught Samantha's attention.

'What is it?' Samantha asked, her voice was weak and raspy but still forceful. Jessica placed the box at the foot of the bed.

'Lord Highcliffe found these as we were getting out some of the party decorations,' she explained, 'he said they might make you feel better?' Picking one of the journals from the box, she blew away the cobwebs, causing her to cough and splutter as she passed it to Samantha. Propping herself upright using her pillows, Samantha looked down at the journal more closely. Jessica was just catching her breath and asked:

'What are they, my lady?'

Samantha was irked by her nosiness; besides, these items were far too personal to share. She waved a hand dismissively.

'Don't you need to prepare for the party?' she stated coldly.

Jessica looked annoyed by the remark and looked poised to offer a comeback, but at the last moment managed to restrain herself as she was in no position to offer a rebuttal. Straitening up, she dusted the cobwebs from her uniform before exiting the room, taking her silent anger with her.

Frankly, Samantha did not like the girl, she was impetuous, ill-mannered and far too fond of prying into things which did not concern her. She was certain Jessica had only got the job as Randell had insisted on interviewing for some of the new staff, and with his wandering eyes, a young beauty like her would have tempted him, of that Samantha had little doubt. Still, with her now dealt with, she could study the box of journals left at the foot of her bed. Running her hand over the cover, she saw that this journal in particular was from her younger days. It had begun as a writing practice tool, forced upon her by her teacher, yet she had come to love writing diaries. Each day she would record the thoughts and feelings that she kept hidden from the outside world.

As she lay in bed, flicking through the diaries and passages sparking half-remembered memories, she came across a passage that reminded her of a time when she was bedridden with illness, much like she is now. She had begun to write in the diary but due to fever, lost the strength to continue. She had fallen asleep for a while and awoke to find one of the older maids, a kindly woman named Anna, sat by her bedside skimming through the journal. Panicked, Samantha had reached out for the diary, Anna shocked by the young girl's sudden movement.

'Give it back… It's not for you…' Samantha had exclaimed through strained breaths. Anna closed the journal and passed it back to her, but a look of sadness had spread across her face. Samantha wretched it from her hands asking:

'Why did you read it?'

Anna looked hurt but replied, 'I merely wanted to get to know more about you, my dear.'

Samantha had been cross: 'A diary is a private thing, I was taught that. It's for the person who writes it, not anyone else.'

Anna smiled, but her eyes remained pools of sadness, 'You are quite right. I apologise.' She paused for a moment before adding, 'I just wish you weren't so…'

Samantha raised an eyebrow curiously, asking:

'Weren't so what?'

Anna sighed, waiting for a moment as if deciding whether to divulge her thoughts. Finally, she spoke.

'Weren't so rude about your father. I know he seems tough, but he means well.'

Samantha folded her arms and reclined back, not looking at Anna as she spoke.

'Father is a brute. You should see what he does to Mother. They think I don't notice but I do. I'm clever, you see. She always appears with bruises whenever they argue. They can't fool me, telling me she fell or tripped or some other excuse. It's clear what he does to her.' Samantha had become more heated as she spoke and stopped only when she began to cough.

Anna pulled her bed covers up and tucked her in gently.

'You may not believe it, but there was a time when your father was kind, full of life and of love. Some years ago, he was full of passions, hopes and dreams.' She paused, as if reminiscing of some happy memory, before her face grew sadder as she continued, 'But time does things to people. He's a man with a reputation you see, and that can put a burden on people. Changes what people expect of you, expect you to do. Sometimes the very thing we want most is the very thing we can't have.' She stopped, turning away for a moment, hiding her face.

Samantha, tucked warmly under the covers, had replied:

'Well, I think that if you want to do something, you should just do it, damn what everyone else says!'

Anna looked back at Samantha and chuckled.

'Ah child, you would think that. One day, when you're much older, you might come to understand.' She leant down and kissed her gently on the forehead. 'For now, rest is what you need.'

Samantha had never come to understand her father, that chance had been taken away by his untimely passing. Samantha had stopped writing diaries once she reached America. She had decided that life was worth living, not to be whiled away writing down one's thoughts and dreams. If you wanted something, you should do it. She had once said. How had it come to pass that she was now trapped in a life she did not want, following what people expected of her? Perhaps, in a roundabout way, she had come to understand her father after all.

Lost in thought, she had not noticed Jessica creep back into the room, still brooding.

'My lady, it's time,' she spoke coolly.

Samantha looked up from the diary in which she had been lost.

'Time for what?' she asked.

Jessica beckoned to the wardrobe.

'The party will be starting soon. We need to get you ready,' Jessica said, aloofly.

Samantha placed the journal back into the box and struggled to stand as she exited the bed, receiving no support from Jessica, who seemed to take pleasure in seeing her Lady struggle. Samantha sighed, regaining her composure and managing to stand upright, despite the exertion it took. People had an expectation of her, and tonight she would live up to those expectations.

XII

Viton begrudgingly walked arm in arm with Madame Cherrie toward Ashbrook, with the sound of music and laughter guiding their way along the darkened path. The pair were arriving late, at Cherrie's request. She justified it to Viton by saying that allowing the party to rage for a while before they would find the guests more inebriated and more open to gossiping once they arrived. However, looking over at her, with lipstick and makeup as alluring as a child's failed face painting, Viton deduced that she had wanted the extra time to "doll" herself up. To the passers-by it would have looked like Viton was arriving with his barmy mother, for the makeup appeared to have aged her rather than having the desired effect. He resolved to lose her at the event as quickly as possible.

The pair arrived at the front doors, held open by two servants who handed them a glass of champagne. They entered into a strange gathering, for it was rare to see such a mixture of people in one place. When Lord Highcliffe had posted his advertisement stating that anyone could come to the party, he clearly hadn't envisioned how far reaching that invite was. It was a smorgasbord of people, in one corner the commoners gathered together and merrily singing, having already consumed too much alcohol, in the middle were the businessmen and women of Melford and in the drawing room were the theatre men and women that Lord Highcliffe intended to woo. They were hidden away, guarded by a row of servants that prevented the riff raff from coming toward them. Occasionally they would look out of the room and grimace or guffaw at the sights of the commoners. Viton and Madame Cherrie found themselves in the middle of all of this, but looking around they could not spot the hosts anywhere.

Cherrie quickly swallowed her glass of champagne and discarded the empty vessel callously on a priceless sideboard.

'Time for us to mingle, I think,' she said, her face reddening. Viton nodded, unsure of what to do with himself, as his presence had been noted by the commoners and business folk, both groups eyeing him with equal distain. Cherrie meanwhile threw herself at Vicar Candour, who looked terrified of the beast before him, particularly in her dress, clearly two sizes too small for her, her breasts almost popped out as she moved.

Viton was watching the spectacle unfold, smirking to himself at the comedic sight, when he felt a firm grip on his shoulder and his arm was forced behind his back, pinning him in an uncomfortable position.

'Hello Viton,' the voice said through gritted teeth. Viton tried to peer over his shoulder, but the vice-like grip upon him tightened.

'Not here.' The voice rasped and with that, he was

pushed out of the entranceway and through the dining room, into a small back corridor that was used by the catering staff. In the cramped, darkened corridor, he was pinned to a wall, his assailant revealing himself as none other than Alfie. His nose was bandaged and two large black circles surrounded his eyes. His pupils were bloodshot but were pinned on Viton with murderous intent.

'Alfie, you're looking well,' Viton said sarcastically.

Alfie grasped Viton tightly by the scuffs of his shirt, his face contorting.

'You think you're so clever, don't ya?' He gestured with one hand to his bandaged face. 'That little stunt hasn't put me off.'

Viton was struggling to get free, but Alfie's grasp was solid.

'Don't think you can get away easy this time. I know what you've been up to, snooping around, calling the office and getting our info from your old buddy. Well, you aren't gunna steal this from me Viton, not now, not ever.' He stopped to catch his breath, 'This is my story, you're old news.'

Viton had relaxed slightly as he knew he couldn't escape Alfie's grasp. He was hoping that a servant would pass by soon, which would give him a chance to slip away. Yet, the longer they stood there, the emptier and lonelier the corridor seemed, the partygoers feeling as if they were miles, not inches, away.

'This is what's gonna happen,' Alfie said, jabbing a

plump finger into Viton's chest. 'Your gunna give me everything you got, and I mean everything.'

Viton wasn't in much position to argue but replied, 'It's all back at the office.'

Alfie scoffed, 'Fine then. Let's go and get it. Now.' He thrust Viton into the doorway and grabbed him again, leading him back through the dining room. Amongst the chattering groups, the drunken merriment and the music, no one noticed Alfie forcefully pushing Viton through the room and looking around, he could not spot Cherrie to ask for aid. Just as it seemed that he was going to be led from the party, a booming voice rang out from the top of the staircase.

'Ladies and gentlemen,' the voice rang out, instantly recognizable as Lord Highcliffe's. Alfie and Viton stopped, both gazing up at his position. He was dressed in a blue and gold suit, the jacket trailing down toward the ground. He waited until the murmuring of the crowd had died down and until he had their undivided attention.

'Thank you for joining us tonight,' he continued, 'and thank you for welcoming us into your humble community. Tonight, we want to show our appreciation by opening up our home to all of you. I want you to enjoy yourselves, be merry, drink and eat to your hearts content and sleep well tonight knowing you have a friend in us.' He paused for a moment looking to his side.

'But now I would like to introduce someone who has yet to show herself to the adoring public, but I'm sure, like me, you'll fall in love with her too.' He gestured to the side and from one of the bedrooms emerged Samantha Highcliffe. She wore a stunning dress, adorned with small encrusted diamonds that glistened like stars in the lights of the Manor, its tight corset emphasizing her slender physique, while the flowing gown gave her an angelic quality. Indeed, her youthful, pale face was one of beauty and innocence, yet she did not smile, rather she remained blank-faced, as if posing for a portrait. For a brief moment, even Viton was taken aback by her visage. At the top of the staircase, she curtsied to the crowd who began to clap and cheer as Lord Highcliffe took her hand and led her slowly down the stairs.

Viton felt adrenaline begin to course through his veins as she neared the crowd, his heart pounding faster with each step she took. Alfie was also enthralled by the unfolding events, unintentionally loosening his grip on Viton. As Lord and Lady Highcliffe reached the insatiable crowd, Viton realised that he was going to lose his chance to talk to the pair if they made their way to the drawing room. He shook Alfie's weakened grip from him and tried to dash forward into the surging crowd.

'Viton!' Alfie yelled, reaching for him, his voice muffled by the claps and cheers of the surrounding crowd. Viton tried to push forward but a wall of people blocked his path and he turned back to face Alfie just as a hefty blow was swung toward him, catching his cheek with a force like a speeding train and knocking him to the ground. Dazed, Viton looked up and saw Alfie, red in the face and ready to grab him, when from behind he was seized by several servants, who wrestled with him for a moment, dragging him away and into the night. Viton could still hear Alfie's angry protests as he disappeared from view. Suddenly, the serving girl, the one he had spoken to previously, appeared, offering him a hand.

'Come on,' she said insistently. Viton's vision was blurred and his head spinning as he grasped her delicate palm and she hauled him up from the hard ground. With all that was going on, few had even noticed the altercation take place, which meant it was easy for the serving girl to lead Viton away from the crowd and into the kitchen. She sat him down on a wooden stool and he leant against the wall as the cooks worked tirelessly, barely even giving his presence a second thought. The girl touched his cheek gently, but it stung and caused Viton to flinch in pain.

'It's really red and swelling. You'll need some ice.' She promptly fetched him a handful of ice cubes, stuffing them into a small bag, which she held to his face. He looked at her thankfully, but she said:

'Take them then, I'm not your nurse.' Viton took over holding the ice, the cool numbing his aching cheek.

'Thank you,' he said genuinely, but the look on the serving girl's face was far from reciprocal.

'I only helped you because I want to know who you are,' she said sternly, 'you obviously aren't on the staff like you told me, because I asked about you after and no one had ever heard of you.'

Viton sighed deeply, gripping the ice a little tighter.

'And now I see you at the party as a guest and in the

middle of a fight no less.'

Viton grimaced.

'It wasn't a fight…' He trailed off. The girl smirked.

'No, you're right, it wasn't. It was you getting your head beat in.' Viton flashed her a scowl.

'So, who are you really?' she said, leaning down close to his face.

Viton sighed, she had helped him, and he didn't see how the truth could hurt.

'I'm a reporter with the local newspaper, I'm writing a story on Lord and Lady Highcliffe and wanted to get to know more about her.'

The girl turned away, nodding and murmuring to herself. Viton was unsure of what he should do, but she turned back with a devilish grin upon her face.

'There's a box of journals upstairs, written by Lady Highcliffe. If you could get those I bet you'd find something for your story.'

Viton looked at her confusedly.

'Why tell me this? Especially after I deceived you.'

The grin had not left her face as she replied, 'Because I hate the Lady and I want you to find out every juicy detail you can about her so that you can smear her name.'

Viton did not disagree with the girl, he too wanted to see an end to the good name of Samantha Highcliffe. He was about to ask her to help him get the journal when another servant appeared calling for her.

'Jessica! Come on, we need your help,' the servant

called into the kitchen.

She leant down and whispered into Viton's ear, 'The journals are in the bedroom, the one she came out of, find a way in and you'll be able to get them. Meet me up there in ten minutes and I can help you get them out.' With that she sauntered off, leaving him to stew. The journals could be invaluable in his quest to understand Samantha Highcliffe and he could only dream of the dirty secrets he could find within. Placing the ice down on the side, his cheek still red and swollen, he made his way out of the kitchen and through the winding corridors back to the main hall.

The party was still raging, and looking into the drawing room, he could see the figures of Lord Highcliffe and Samantha surrounded by admiring guests. They were like birds flocking around discarded bread, desperate for any crumbs that would be thrown their way. Stumbling out of the crowd, Cherrie collapsed into Viton's arms, stinking of booze. He hadn't been gone that long, but she had clearly drunken herself into a stupor.

'What happened to you?' she slurred at him, placing her hand onto his cheek, which he shook off. Her makeup looked even more horrific, if that was possible, as it was rubbed in all manner of directions across her face. From across the room, Viton was shocked to see the gaunt figure of Mr Brindle, his face covered with Cherrie's smeared lipstick. He raised his glass of champagne in Viton's direction, smiling sadistically. Viton wanted to confront him, but Cherrie clung to him unsteadily, holding him in place and by the time he glanced back, Brindle had already disappeared into the crowd.

'I said,' Cherrie exclaimed loudly, but slowly, 'what happened to you?'

Pushing the thought of Brindle from his mind he muttered roughly, 'It doesn't matter.' Before saying more quietly, 'I've got a lead, I need to get upstairs.' Cherrie looked at him confused, she was clearly not following and drifting in and out of sleep. However, her drunken demeanour gave him an idea. Carrying her over to the staircase, he was stopped by a servant.

'Upstairs is for the Lord and Lady or staff only, sir,' he said, blocking their way.

'I understand, it's just my friend here is a bit of a state, and she thinks she's going to vomit, I don't want to alarm you, but the que for the bathroom down here is immense, she's likely to upchuck all over the good Lord and Lady's valuables. I was hoping we could just get her upstairs until she's sobered up a bit.'

Cherrie looked up at the servant and he almost recoiled at her appearance.

'Good gosh,' he exclaimed. 'She looks dreadful, we better get her upstairs.' He moved and wrapped Cherrie's other arm around his shoulder. He and Viton carried her limp body up the stairs and out of sight of the rest of the partygoers. They entered a small lavatory and deposited her by the toilet bowl as she sprawled herself across it. The servant rushed off to get some water and Viton watched as he headed down the stairs. When he was out of sight, Viton slipped away, leaving Cherrie where she lay and heading across to the bedroom. He twisted the door handle slowly and slid into the room, closing it quietly behind him.

Inside, Viton could see a variety of discarded outfits and makeup pallets and brushes strewn around the room. The beauty had been achieved through a heavy handed application of these tools, Viton deduced. Looking around, he spotted the box of journals, as the serving girl had said, at the bedside. They were illuminated by the light of the pale moon shinning in through the stain glass windows. Viton hurried over to the box and picked up the first of the leather-bound journals, opening the front cover. The dates aligned with the months in which he had been covering the murder of her parents and in that moment everything else was forgotten – the party, the Manor, Brindle – everything fell from his mind as he scoured the pages looking for the date the act had been committed. He came to rest on the page, in which he could see the date scrawled in shaky handwriting.

He was just about to read the entry when a bloodcurdling scream echoed around the house and through the halls. Tucking the journal under his jacket quickly, he rushed out onto the balcony and could see the partygoers watching as Lord Highcliffe carried his wife in his arms. Her skin was like a corpse, strewn in his arms, limp and lifeless, if it had not been for the flashes of her horror-stricken eyes, Viton would have assumed she was dead. Realizing they were fighting through the crowd to reach the staircase, Viton hurried to collect Cherrie from the bathroom.

'Viton?' She looked up from the toilet bowl that she was sprawled across, bleary eyed. Saying nothing, he picked her up and opened the bathroom door a fraction, allowing Lord Highcliffe and a swath of servants to make their way to the bedroom before he snuck out, using the confusion to sneak down the stairs. Given the commotion, Viton and Cherrie slipped away without much notice, the journal still tucked tightly under his jacket. As they escaped the Manor into the cold, bellowing night air, shrieks and shrills behind them, Cherrie clawed at his chest and said:

'Viton, what happened back there?'

Viton kept on walking, he wasn't sure what had happened to Samantha Highcliffe, all he knew was that in his jacket he held the key to unlocking the truth of a mystery that had hung over his life like a shadow. He marched on into the night, more determined than ever

XIII

After several wardrobe changes and tubs of makeup being applied, Samantha could stand to look at herself in the mirror. Her weary complexion was hidden away behind layers of varying products and this made her feel able to play the part of doting host. Standing up, she twirled her dress, the diamonds dazzling her in the reflection of the mirror. As she was finishing readying herself, Randell entered the room. Jessica curtsied to him, smiling sweetly, but he ignored her and headed straight to Samantha.

'My darling, you look exquisite!' He proclaimed, placing his warm hands onto her cold, exposed shoulders. The sensation was pleasing to Samantha and she allowed his hands to remain there.

'You think so?' Samantha asked coyly.

'My dear, the whole town will be entranced with your beauty! You are like an angel sent from above!' Randell professed dramatically. By the door, Jessica scoffed quietly, unnoticed by Randell but not by Samantha.

'You'd better be off,' Samantha barked at her. 'There are plenty of jobs you could be doing.'

Jessica slipped silently from the room. Randell eyed his wife mockingly.

'Come come, my dear, there is no need for such coldness tonight. You must play the part of the adoring host, you have the look, now I need to see the attitude.'

Samantha shook his hands from her shoulders in response to this comment, turning to face him with dogged determination.

'I believe, dear.' She paused for effect, 'That this party was your idea. Do not lecture me on how best to behave. I will do as I have always done, play the part of the socialite. When all this is over, I expect we shall talk about how best to go forward, with my interests at heart. Not just yours.'

Randell looked concerned and tugged at the neck of his collar.

'Of course dear, of course!' He said dismissively, 'For now, let us join the dreamer's downstairs!'

Samantha sighed, once again, her thoughts and feelings seemed to fall upon deaf ears. She seemed forever destined to be trapped in a cage of her own making, at the mercy of others wants and dreams. Randell had rushed from the room and had positioned himself at the top of the staircase, delivering a speech of some grandeur in his usual flamboyant way. Suddenly, it was her turn to emerge, her legs shook and felt weak beneath her, she couldn't decide if this was due to the illness afflicting her or nerves at the sight of the gawping crowd. She emerged from the bedroom slowly, she could not walk much faster for fear of over exerting herself, yet as she moved forward, the crowd gazed up at her adoringly. Samantha kept a blank face, for she knew of the fickle nature of people, one moment they would love her, the next they would slander her. She reached Randell and he took her hand, the pair slowly descending down the staircase. The crowd was surging and reaching toward the two as if they were angels descending from heaven, but Samantha felt her skin crawl as she pictured them as rats, gnawing at her flesh.

As they reached the bottom of the staircase, the crowd all clamoured to get her attention, reaching for her, feeling for her, but Randell and a group of servants kept them at bay as the two made their way to the drawing room to join the other members of higher society. The sounds, the sights, the atmosphere was overwhelming and Samantha felt as if her head were being slowly tightened in a vice. Yet, just as quickly as the pressure exerted itself, it relaxed as the two reached the drawing room, allowing them some space to breathe.

'Goodness, they adore you,' said an unknown woman, saddling up to Samantha. She was older than her, the wrinkles told that story, but she still had an air of elegance and grace about her.

'Of course they adore her!' Randell exclaimed from beside her, 'All you have to do is look at her to know she's a diamond!'

The woman smiled wryly at Samantha. 'I think we all know that looks aren't everything, the mind too can be a wonderful thing.'

Randell looked slightly embarrassed and spluttered, 'Well yes, yes, of course!' He had gone slightly red-faced, and spotting a theatre owner that he recognized from his previous trip into the town, he hastened to join him and escape the company of two strong women.

Samantha smiled at the woman, offering her name and inquiring as to hers.

'Ah, I'm Mrs Brindle,' she replied, still smiling. Samantha nodded absently, remembering her encounter with the tempestuous Mr Brindle.

'I can see from the look on your face dear, that you don't think much of my husband,' she said, taking a swig of champagne from the flute she held in her hand. Chuckling as she spoke, she added, 'Don't worry, I don't think much either.'

Samantha couldn't help but smirk at this comment, as the two women wandered over to the window, away from the other gawking guests who were surrounding Randell. He was in the middle of a speech about his favourite painting, the warrior fighting the lion, and Samantha dreaded to think of the crass comments he would be making. In her mind, it was better to be out of earshot and with a woman who seemingly understood what it was like to be trapped with someone who didn't live up to the opinion you once held.

The two women stood for a moment, looking out into the darkness, allowing the noise and merriment of the party to fade into the background as they enjoyed a moment of solitude. Mrs Brindle spoke first, while brushing dust from the ancient windows off her dress. It was plain in appearance, one that would have been commonly available, yet Samantha found this didn't detract from her class.

'How are you liking the place?'

Samantha glanced around at the room, as if it was her first time properly examining it.

'It's nice,' she replied.

Mrs Brindle guffawed, 'Just nice? This place is magnificent!'

Samantha looked uncertainly at her and then looked over at Randell as the crowd around him erupted into fits of laughter, as if they were crows squawking in unison. Mrs Brindle caught her sideward glance.

'Ah, I'm not sure the issue lies with this house,' she said, knowingly. Samantha remained stoic, not allowing her face to show any emotion.

'I understand, my dear,' the woman said, placing a soothing hand onto Samantha's forearm. 'Sometimes we find ourselves in these situations where what we thought was good once has lost its lustre. As does the body fade with time, so does love.' She looked at her own withered palm at this point resentfully. 'One grows used to the circumstance, it can be hard to see a way forward. You learn to make do with what you have and enjoy what little you can.' There was a long silence as she finished speaking, as if everything around them had faded from existence and it was just the two of them left standing there, both trapped in their misery.

Samantha looked at her closely, it was as if she could read her mind, understand her thoughts, even better than she could. She went to open her mouth, to speak, to divulge all that she felt and to confirm that all she had said was true, but before she could the older woman had placed a finger to her lips.

'Some things are better left unsaid,' she uttered quietly, her eyes flickered over her shoulder, and looking back, Samantha saw the maid, Jessica stood nearby, pretending not to listen. Samantha hadn't even seen her enter the room, that was how engrossed she was in Mrs Brindle's presence. Leading her by the arm further from the serving girl, Mrs Brindle spoke again.

'You might be wondering why my interest in your opinion of this place. It wasn't just idle chatter, myself and my husband own this property,' she explained, a smug grin spreading over her face.

Samantha was taken aback that someone of such common appearance as her was the owner of such a property, particularly given the meek presence of Mr Brindle when she had met him.

'You own this place?' Samantha asked.

Mrs Brindle smiled. 'Don't look so shocked, dear!'

Samantha blushed, the red tint penetrating through the thick makeup plastered to her cheeks.

'I apologise. Your husband didn't say anything when he showed us in.'

Mrs Brindle shook her head. 'Oh, he wouldn't, the man's a coward at heart,' she said coldly. 'The truth is we've fallen on some… hard times lately, hence the letting of the house.'

Samantha almost felt sorry for her as she spoke, both that

she was married to a man like Brindle and for her circumstance.

'Did you live here then?' Samantha asked curiously.

Mrs Brindle raised her eyebrows. 'Oh, for a time...' she trailed off as if lost in thought.

The pair had come to rest at the far end of the drawing room, beside a window, looking out into the night once more. The dark seemed somehow infinite now, and the howling of the menacing wind was growing louder. Samantha found herself growing more curious as to how much she knew about the house, questions flooded her mind, images of her encounters on the previous night's raging.

'Did you ever see anything... strange while you were living here?' Samantha said cautiously.

As if waking from a dream, Mrs Brindle looked up, meeting her gaze, a deathly serious look had overtaken her face.

'Strange?' she repeated. 'What do you mean strange?'

Samantha felt unable to look away, and suddenly Mrs Brindle had begun to squeeze her arm more tightly, causing her to flinch in pain.

'Mrs Brindle...' Samantha said, trying to tug her arm away. Mrs Brindle remained steadfast, repeating again.

'What do you mean strange?' Her grip was becoming tighter, her fingers beginning to dig into Samantha's skin.

'Mrs Brindle!' Samantha squealed slightly louder.

Suddenly, Mr Brindle appeared behind his wife and despite his smaller stature, dragged her off and away.

Samantha stared down at her skin, the nail marks red and raw. The pair exchanged a low set of heated words before Mr Brindle approached Samantha, his face bizarrely covered in makeup.

'I must apologise Lady Highcliffe, my wife can suffer from these bouts of hysteria from time to time.' He waited, but Samantha looked at him, unsatisfied with the answer. Stumbling over his words, he continued, 'I can only apologise, and well, I suppose we'll leave at once,' he finished. Samantha nodded curtly, rubbing her arm tenderly and turning away from them. She heard the pair making a noisy exit behind her, but didn't dare look back.

Was she going mad? The woman had clearly become deranged at the mention of anything odd happening at the Manor. Perhaps she too had seen the strange figures, the rooms which appeared and disappeared seemingly in an instant, or that haunting old maid who had slipped into Samantha's bedroom. Was she destined to end up like Mrs Brindle? The thought made her shudder, and she suddenly felt herself growing weaker. The strain of the physical exertion was beginning to affect her.

She slumped against the window, wearily. However, as she looked out, she was shocked to see two pairs of white eyes staring back at her through the glass. Out there, in the cold of night, the shadowy creatures lurked, watching her. In terror, she recoiled, letting out a bloodcurdling screech and falling backward to the floor, her body convulsing uncontrollably. Randell pushed his way past the onlookers that promptly gathered around her and picked her limp body up from the floor. She was deathly cold, she could hardly move and her vision was blurring. Griping her tightly, Randell forced his way back to the staircase, a bevy of servants following him and holding back the worried guests. She was rushed into her bedroom, placed beneath the covers and the doctor summoned promptly. It did not take long for him to appear, as he had been attending the party and with help, he managed to get Samantha to swallow a sleeping draught. Samantha had no conception of what was happening, all she could see was the haunting white eyes and the shadows swirling around her.

Randell watched as his wife's wild eyes calmed, her body becoming still beneath the sheets. Slowly, her eyes drooped shut, for what would be the last time.

XIV

Viton surged onward, Cherrie still draped over him, as they battled through the bitter winds to reach the newspaper office. The journey had been slow, with Viton having to stop at several points to recover his strength, meanwhile his brain was raging with thoughts, ideas and wonders. He knew the journal would have the answers, it had to.

He had never been so grateful to see the office coming into view as the pair finally neared its welcoming walls. However, as they reached the entrance, Viton was shocked to see the front door wide open, swinging backward and forward in the wind. For a brief moment he thought Cherrie may have left it that way before the party, but as he looked closer, it was clear that the door had been forced open. The lock and hinges were splintered, someone had broken it open with considerable force. As he poked his head into the entranceway, he heard a repeated banging noise, echoing from upstairs. Viton placed Cherrie down just inside the building, fearing that the intruder might still be present. Reaching inside his jacket, he retrieved the valued journal and tucked it under Cherrie's limp arms for safekeeping. With that, he began to creep down the hall toward the stairs, each step carefully considered as to not make too much noise.

Reaching the stairs, he looked up, hoping to see if anyone was present, but from where he was he couldn't see into the office. Bang, bang, bang. The noise continued, as if in rhythm, like a drumbeat through the building. Viton placed a foot onto the first step, unsurely. Should he call for help? But who would be around at this time, and with everyone up at the Manor for the party, he wasn't certain anyone would come anyway. The best thing seemed to be to investigate for himself. Still, he moved slowly up the stairs, hoping the noise would stop, but it carried on all the same. Reaching the top of the stairs, Viton shuffled to the doorway and risked a quick glance in. He couldn't see anyone. Rounding the corner, he breathed a sigh of relief as he saw the far window was open, the pane swinging backward and forward, creating the banging noise. This wasn't the only thing though. The office was a total mess, papers thrown all around the room, desk drawers opened and tossed aside, clearly whoever had got in was looking for something.

Closing the window and freeing himself of the dreaded banging, Viton returned to collect Cherrie and the journal, propping the front door closed as best he could. The pair headed upstairs and Viton laid her down on a bed of newspapers. She was fast asleep within minutes, leaving him to sit and take stock of the carnage that had been rendered onto the office. The floor was carpeted with pages of notes, folders and discarded newspaper clippings and Viton's desk was missing drawers that had seemingly been tossed aside. He noticed immediately that all of his notes surrounding

Samantha Highcliffe were missing, as was the documentation about Ashbrook Manor he had procured from the public records building.

Slamming his fist on his desk angrily, Viton cursed himself. He was sure this was the work of Alfie, he should have known that he wouldn't have given up the chase that easily. If he had been smarter, he would never have revealed where all his work was kept and the office would not have ended up in such a state. Taking a deep breath, he sighed before reassuring himself as he retrieved the journal from beside Cherrie and placed it onto his desk. He smiled to himself, almost maniacally.

Alfie may have had his notes, but in the end, it wouldn't matter as with this journal, Viton was certain he was going to be able to finally bring an end to Samantha Highcliffe. He opened the journal and as Cherrie slept silently, began to pour over the contents, searching for the truth hidden within.

XV

It was on a day like any other that Samantha's life had changed. The breeze was gently blowing through the open window, the sunlight streaming in. She had been staring absentmindedly out of the window, work set by her tutor hardly comparing to the glistening green vistas on view just over the estate walls. It was at a moment like that she wished she could paint and capture the sight, to relive it over and over. Yet the beauteous image was shattered by the loud shouts of her father, booming from his office. He was locked in another argument with her mother, a sound Samantha had grown accustomed to as it was the symphony of her childhood and adolescence.

The argument seemed to rage for some time, but it was when she heard her name mentioned that her curiosity was piqued. At first, she had tried to listen by leaning out of the open window, but the whispered tones of her mother were lost over the deafening yells of her father, so she decided to creep down the corridor to better listen. Arriving at the grand office door, Samantha knelt down, her knees resting on the cold marble flooring and tilting her head, peered through the keyhole. She sat as quietly as she could while she listened.

'Don't you think it's time we let the girl go?' her mother said, sat feebly in a chair in front of her father's antique desk, lined with various trinkets from his travels. Her father was sat on the far side his desk, a cigar within his mouth. From their positions, it was as if her mother were an employee meeting with her manager, not like a discussion between wife and husband at all. From her view she could see her father chomp hard on the end of his cigar before he spoke.

'IF,' he began loudly before suddenly realizing the window was open and hastening to shut it. After he had fastened it, he returned to his desk, leaning with two palms pressed upon it, her mother becoming like a shrinking violet beneath his domineering stance. 'If,' he said more quietly, but in nonetheless a more commanding tone, 'if we send her away, then you know what will happen. To us, to you. There would be talk, rumour, gossip. It's served us well to have her within these walls all these years.'

'It has served you well, you mean,' her mother retorted without pausing for a moment to think. The look of panic that shot across her face as the words left her mouth showed that she wished she had thought. Her father pointed an angry finger toward her, barking:

'Mind your tongue, woman. If you know what's good for you.'

Immediately, her mother shrunk back in her seat. Samantha hated her father and the beastly attitude he showed toward her mother. Samantha prayed she would not be on the end of another beating after that comment, but mercifully her father had resumed his seat in solemn contemplation.

Suddenly, Samantha became aware of another presence watching over her and turned to see the maid Anna peering at her with a grin on her face.

'And what would you be doing, madam?' she asked knowingly.

Samantha sprung up from her position on the floor, dusting her red and cold knees.

'I was just... I...' Samantha couldn't come up with a believable excuse.

'I know exactly what you were doing madam. Off with you! These conversations are not for prying eyes and ears!' Anna shoed her away in a jovial manner. She watched closely as Samantha slowly traipsed back up the corridor toward her room, glancing back from time to time. As the voices became raised, Anna opened the office door with a look of worry upon her face, allowing Samantha the chance to rush back to her viewing spot. Peering back through the keyhole, she saw Anna approaching timidly as her father had his back to the doorway and her mother sat, arms folded.

'Is there anything I can do to be of assistance, sir?' Anna looked to her father. However, Samantha was shocked to see the look of anger that had flooded her mother's reddened face.

'I think you've done enough, don't you?' she spat venomously.

Her father turned around to face the two women and held up a solitary hand.

'That's enough, dear,' he said, coldly.

Suddenly, her mother had risen from the chair. 'No, I don't think it is enough dear. That's the problem, nothing has ever been enough for you. That's why we've ended up in this situation, that's why things went wrong for us. If you'd been content, if I'd been enough, then you'd have never... with her...' She pointed her finger at Anna disgustedly. Samantha would never fully understand the pent-up anger, shame, and hatred that had been festering in her mother's heart all those years, but it was at this moment that it finally erupted with the might of a volcano, and she struck Anna with a flat palm across the face. An almighty crack rang across the room.

'Good god woman!' Her father yelled as he rushed to cradle Anna.

'No! I've had enough, putting up with this all these years, this bitch allowed to roam free within my house when I know what she's done! What she's caused!' Her mother yelled, lunging forward at the pair.

She grabbed the scruffs of Anna's outfit and began to wrestle with her, appearing to have truly gone mad. As the pair tussled, Anna, the younger and fitter of the two, shoved her with great force. Her mother tumbled backward and struck her head upon the corner of desk with a chilling crunch. Samantha looked on, horror-stricken, as her mother lay on the floor, a thick puddle of blood seeping onto the carpeted floor. Without thinking, Samantha wrenched the door open and rushed into the room, crashing past Anna and her father who both stood horrified.

'Mother! Mother!' Samantha cried, shaking her lifeless body. Her hands became reddened from the blood pouring onto the floor. Behind her, her father began to shake with rage.

'I'm sorry...' Anna spoke hauntedly as Samantha began

to weep for her mother.

With powerful, bear-like hands, Samantha's Father seized Anna, wrapping his hands tightly around her delicate throat, squeezing the life from her. 'If it wasn't for you!' He yelled maniacally, 'life would have been perfect; she would still be alive!'

Samantha recoiled at the scene, tumbling over her mother's body.

'Please! Stop this! Please!' She yelled, to no avail. Her father was a powerful man, hulking in his fury and showed no signs of stopping until Anna drew her last breath. She was gasping for air as Samantha rushed forward, grabbing at her father's broad shoulders. He released Anna with one hand and swung back wildly, striking Samantha across the face with a hefty blow, sending her sprawling backward. Samantha's vision was blurred, but she saw the respite she had given Anna had allowed her to pick up the paperweight again, and this time deliver a violent swing, straight across the temple of her father. The sound was almost unhuman as her father sprawled limply in front of her, withering as the colour began to drain from him, his blood mixing with that of her mother's and coating the floor. He seemed to be trying to utter something, but before he could, his eyes receded into the back of his head and he became deathly still.

For a moment, both she and Anna exchanged silent glances, unsure of what to do, taking a moment to comprehend what had just happened. Samantha struggled to her feet as Anna looked horrified at the heavy paperweight she held, its edges smeared with a thick red liquid. Samantha looked down in disbelief, her father lay with a cold expression frozen on his face, his skin a murky grey. Anna dropped the bloodied instrument to the floor with a thud and quickly embraced Samantha, cradling and stroking her hair as tears ran down her face.

'I didn't mean to… I just wanted him to stop…' She uttered heartbrokenly. Samantha looked down hopelessly. Both her mother and father lay cold and dead on the ground. It seemed cruel that on such a beautiful day, such darkness had been unleashed, leading to this. Lost, and suddenly all alone in the world, Samantha had no idea what to do except to sob into Anna's chest.

'Come with me, child,' Anna said, tears also running down her face. She took Samantha's hand and lead her down the corridor away from the grim reality and back to her room. First, she commanded they both wash the smeared ruby blood from their hands. Next, she gave Samantha a change of clothes before pulling a suitcase from the shelf, which she began to pour other clothes into it.

'What are you doing?' Samantha said confused, undressing quickly.

'We have to leave,' Anna responded resolutely.

'We?' Samantha questioned. 'My parents are dead and you want me to leave with you?' She was flabbergasted. Anna ignored her questions and continued to pack the bag until Samantha finished changing, coming forward and shaking her arm. 'What is going on?' she said, lost in the dizzying, unfolding events. It was like being in a bizarre dream, except this time, there was no waking up.

Anna knelt down slightly and met her gaze intensely. Droplets of blood were still splattered across her face. 'There are things you don't know. About your family. About yourself. But this isn't the time, my dear. We must go. Soon there will be answers, I promise. But not now.' And so, like a lost sheep, under the guidance of Anna, the pair packed bags and slipped off, out of the walls of the estate and across the sunlit hills, walking for what seemed like hours, not stopping to talk, always moving. Samantha had dreamed about leaving the estate and being free, but never imagined it would have been like this.

They reached the seaside town, and the two women booked into a small hotel, sharing a meagre room between them. Once alone, Samantha felt it was the time for answers. Anna sighed and sat upon the bed, her eyes full of sorrow and regret. She spun a tale for Samantha, painted an image of many years past when her father had been younger, virile and a man of a caring disposition. Yet the man was frivolous and he enjoyed the company of many women. One of these women was Anna, the pair had spent many nights together. She did not love him, but she admired him, his position and his power. Yet he would not leave his wife for her. It would be ludicrous for a man of his wealth to divorce and marry a common maid, even Anna knew this. She submitted to playing the humble role of maid by day, mistress by night. Unfortunately, this all came crashing down around her when she found she was pregnant. At first, she wanted to rid herself of the problem, but the child's father had convinced her otherwise, for there was a chance he would have a male heir that his wife had yet to provide. Thus, the three conspired. It took some "convincing" (as Anna called it) but her father, mother and Anna all swore to never reveal the truth. Anna would birth a son for the family and they would pass him off as their own. Samantha's mother was never entirely happy with the situation, but Anna described this as being the time that her parents changed. Her father became cruel, bending his wife to his whim in order to protect his own fragile façade of virtue. However, nine months later, when the time came for the child to be born, the plan almost unravelled as a girl was born instead.

'You,' Anna said, pointed toward Samantha. 'You were born, Samantha. Sadly, you bore my looks.'

Samantha looked in the mirror and then closely at Anna. The likeness was noticeable, yet years of conditioning had meant she never questioned her parentage. Now the reason why she was not to leave the estate became clear, the question which had hung over her, unanswered for her entire life, was finally answered.

'Now, you understand, my dear?' She reached out a hand and took Samantha's cold, pale palm in her own. Samantha did. It all fit too perfectly to not be true. She was an unwanted child, a problem, locked away, a prisoner to be dealt with. A million thoughts raged through her mind as the women readied themselves to try to sleep. Samantha lay awake, staring uncertainly at the woman who was in fact her mother. For years, she had slaved away beneath her, always watching, always waiting. Yet, for Samantha, she hardly knew her, had barely cared to learn about her and found herself feeling nothing for her. She might as well have been a stranger, laying across asleep in her bed.

It was in that dark night, laying alone in the bedroom, that twisted thoughts entered her mind. One in which she could be free of her prison, of the burden of 'Samantha Highcliffe'. That night, she retrieved her suitcase, and while Anna slept, she stole away into the dark, buying passage on a boat to America with what little money she had. It was time for her to start a new life. Free of everyone and everything, she knew before.

***

Suddenly back within her bedroom, tears filled Samantha's eyes and she wept tears of bitter sorrow in the pervading darkness. She had grown up, living a lie, wearing the face of a Highcliffe. Trapped within the walls of the family estate and within the very fibre of her being. Her short-lived trip to America was the one time she was free, when she had cast off the shroud of the Highcliffe's and lived for herself as herself. Yet in the end, she had wound up back wearing that dreaded mask and she could bear it no longer.

She cried and cried until she felt her eyes grow raw and her throat hoarse. Without warning, comforting hands began to gently caress her back. Looking up, she saw the face of the old maid – that same terrifying figure which had haunted her room two nights prior. However, the horror Samantha had felt before was fading away, despite the skeletal presence's disconcerting looks.

'Mother?' Samantha said, her voice wavering.

The woman smiled sweetly and opened her arms for an embrace, just as she had the previous night. This time Samantha threw herself into the woman's body and buried her head deep within her chest, wrapping her arms around her tightly. The pair hugged each other comfortingly. Despite her appearance, a healing warmth radiated from her.

'You've been through such hardships, my dear,' the old woman spoke, her voice like a lullaby, ushering Samantha to rest.

'Now it's time to be free of your burdens,' she said calmly. Samantha held her tightly, acceptingly, and felt her eyes flickering as she could no longer resist the urge to close them. Peacefully, she embraced the never-ending dark of sleep and found herself in an eternal dream, one where she was finally free. The dream she had yearned for all her life, come true.

At her bedside, the shadowy creatures stood and watched as a peaceful smile came over their prey as she slept soundly. Somewhere within the grand Manor, the chiming of a clock echoed through the halls, reaching out into the fading darkness. The dawn of a new morning was about to break.

XVI

The moonless night had passed and dawn broken, but Viton had not slept. He had been enthralled by the narrative unfolding within Samantha's journal and poured over the entries at least three or four times. Now, sleep deprived and weary, he slumped back in his chair, unable to comprehend what he had read on those fragile pages. Everything he believed about Samantha Highcliffe was wrong and this shook him to his very core. For over a year he had harboured a festering hatred, a desire for revenge and a cynical view of those around him, yet, now, it seemed it was all for nothing. Despair crept into his mind, like a looming shadow. He would have wept if his eyes weren't so dry.

All at once he was overwhelmed with feelings of shame and disgust, as memories flashed through his mind rapidly, images of the shaken Lee, Alfie bloodied at his own hands, his theft of the papers from the records office. Then he remembered the sickly Samantha Highcliffe that he had seen just hours before. Pale, weak and deathly. The look on her face haunted him, and he could not rid himself of it even when he closed his eyes. Before reading the diary, he would not have cared what happened to her, but now he saw the truth, he couldn't help but pity her. By reading the entry, he had figured out what had happened all that time ago. The maid Anna had tricked him. He remembered her as clear as day and the descriptions from within the diary matched all perfectly with his memory. It was she who had told him that Samantha had murdered her parents before disappearing herself, which had led to him publishing the story, with his witness then appearing to be fabricated. No doubt she had deceived him to cover her own back or to spite Samantha for abandoning her. He doubted he would ever find her again now, even if she were still alive, so he would never know for certain. Looking down, he examined his rough hands. He needed to make amends for what he had done, and there was only one way he could see himself doing that. He grabbed the typewriter from the far side of his desk and began to hammer furiously on the keys.

The sun hung low in the sky as he finished the article. Pulling the paper from the typewriter, he looked it over contently. He now had three perfect copies of the article ready. It was to be a celebration of Samantha Highcliffe, of her life and her triumphant arrival in Melford. Viton was ready to make amends in any way he could. Picking up his jacket, he readied himself to leave, one copy left on the desk of Madame Cherrie, who was only just beginning to stir. Packing the two other copies and the journal into a bag, Viton smiled and nodded to himself, he finally felt he was doing the right thing after fumbling in the dark of hatred for so long.

Pulling on his coat as he left the office, he tucked the bag tightly under his arm as he marched towards Ashbrook

Manor. It wasn't a long walk from the office and he marched forward with purpose. He was going to show Samantha Highcliffe the article and apologise to her personally. Even if she didn't know who he was, he felt she ought to know the person who had started the besmirching of her name and he needed the chance to make things right. In some way, if he could convince her to forgive him, perhaps he could have some kind of redemption.

Walking the cobbled streets, he stopped at the post box, labelling and stuffing a copy of the article inside. He might have failed to find out about Ashbrook Manor, but he hoped that Eddie would instead consider publishing his article about Samantha. The least he could do was try. With only one copy left to show the titular lady, he journeyed onward, hoping she could find it somewhere in her heart to forgive him. There was also the awkward matter of the journal, but he hoped that his kind words, transcribed on the page, would be enough to forgive him his faults. After all, the words he had written would live forever.

He walked almost in a daze up to the house, its looming presence blocking out the morning sun, casting deep shadows onto the ground. Standing in the chill, Viton reached his hand out toward the door and found himself trembling slightly. It was only slight, for he knew more than ever what he had to do, but still he couldn't help feeling dread in the pit of his stomach. It was never easy to admit you were wrong or to make amends for discretions committed years prior. His hand came to rest on the doorknob and he took a resolute, deep breath. He knocked firmly, the sound ringing out around him.

The door was pulled open with surprising ferocity, that startled Viton. Lord Highcliffe was there, looking fraught, the colour drained from him and large black bags hung beneath his eyes, almost weighing down his entire face.

'You aren't the doctor!' He cried, a mixture of confusion and despair in his voice.

'No, I'm not,' Viton said, 'has something happened, Lord Highcliffe?'

'My wife... my wife...' Lord Highcliffe spouted unsurely.

'I actually came to see your wife, Lord Highcliffe, you see...' Viton reached into his bag to retrieve his article, but his arm was suddenly tightly seized by Lord Highcliffe.

'You don't understand...' he said, shaking his head solemnly. 'My wife... I fear she is...' he trailed off, relaxing his grip.

Viton looked back at him, confused. 'Show me,' he said commandingly. It might have been the force with which he spoke or Lord Highcliffe's despairing nature, but he relented and allowed Viton in. Following Lord Highcliffe indoors, Viton found the house was still in a state of disrepair from the party the previous night. It looked as if the house had been ransacked, things were missing from their place, ornaments smashed on the ground, as well as drinks flutes. Lord Highcliffe seemed unfazed and simply lead Viton on.

'Where are the staff, Lord Highcliffe?' Viton said as they walked carefully over the broken deluge.

'Just up and abandoned us! I can't find them anywhere, not a trace!' He called back. The pair reached the stairs and made their way upstairs, entering the bedroom Viton had seen Samantha be carried into the night before.

Inside, the sun was shining through the stain glass, creating a rainbow of colour that lit up the bed Samantha lay in. Lord Highcliffe knelt at her bedside and clutched one hand with both of his, not daring to look at her face. Viton saw her lying there, peaceful, with a sweet, contented smile upon her face. As he approached, he dug the article from his bag, ready to show her, but as he neared, he saw why Lord Highcliffe was fearful. Despite the contented look on her face, her skin was a lifeless shade of grey. Reaching out, Viton touched her free hand gently. It felt as if it were frostbitten. He placed two fingers on her wrist to feel for a pulse, but found none. Samantha Highcliffe was dead. His great chance at redemption, of making amends, like smoke in the wind, had vanished.

He looked over at Lord Highcliffe, who was gazing up at him, pitifully. Viton grimaced and shook his head. Lord Highcliffe let go of his wife's hand, allowing it to drop gracefully back into place on the bed, before he walked slowly over to Viton, suddenly embracing him and burying his head into his chest, starting to sob violently. It wasn't common for a man to show such emotion, but seeing as he had just lost everyone and everything he held dear, Viton did not resist. Instead, he stood, an empty shell of a man, unable to find solace as his chance to redeem himself slipped away.

After a few moments of sobbing, Lord Highcliffe, still not lifting his head, asked:

'Did you know my wife well?' The question hung in the putrid air for a moment before Viton found the strength to answer.

'No, I don't think I ever really did,' Viton answered solemnly. It was true, Viton had spent years hating Samantha for crimes she did not commit and events that happened to him, of which she had no control over. Now, only when he came to discover the truth was it too late to get to know the real Samantha. The article was still awkwardly held in his hand, weighing heavily upon him.

He was about to hand it to Lord Highcliffe when something over his crying frame caught his eye. The stain glass window, through which the light radiated, looked as if it depicted a woman eerily similar to Samantha within her bed. Viton looked backward and forward between the window and the bed, the details were almost exactly the same.

'Lord Highcliffe,' Viton said, about to show him the stain glass. He looked up but did not let go of Viton.

Suddenly from behind they heard the creaking of the bedroom door. Lord Highcliffe released Viton and both men looked over to the doorway. In the frame stood the small, menacing figure of Mr Brindle. He sighed and shut the door quietly behind him.

EPILOGUE

It was a bright morning, the sun blazing in through the shop windows as I sat at my desk, blankly filling in the papers. Normally such good weather would fill the townsfolk with cheer, but a solemn gloom seemed to have overtaken all of us after the events at the party. My head was still hurting, for what had begun as a night of merriment and revelry ended in confusion and despair. I hoped Samantha Highcliffe was all right. After all, she had looked so beautiful but somehow fragile, like a glass figurine, as if the smallest knock could have shattered her. I suppose I would find out soon enough, Mr Brindle had left a message to say he was at the Manor to check on her that morning, as he felt it was his place. I hadn't actually managed to speak to Mr Brindle since before the party and the document Viton had shown me still lingered in the back of my mind, like a candle, slowly burning. That was something else to ask about.

With that thought still percolating, the door to the agency shot open and Mr Brindle hurried past quickly, carrying papers and some kind of journal beneath his arm. He didn't even glance my way, so I stood up and yelled:

'Well?' Just as he reached the door to his office. He came to a shuddering halt before glancing back and saying:

'You better come in.'

I followed him into the office quickly, eager to find out the news. I sat down in the chair opposite him as he sat down and placed the papers and journal onto his antique desk, just in front of me.

He rubbed his eyes, wearily, before saying:

'I'm afraid Samantha Highcliffe is dead.' The news was like a shot through the heart as I stared back disbelievingly.

'What? How? She was so young...' I trailed off into quiet contemplation.

Mr Brindle cleared his throat before continuing.

'Well, the doctor was there when I left, so no doubt we'll find out in time what caused it.'

I sat for a moment quietly contemplating, but then something caught my eye on the table. The paperwork that Mr Brindle had placed down, it appeared to be an article written by Viton. Looking up, Mr Brindle seemed to have caught my prying gaze and was staring back with a look of displeasure on his face.

'Something wrong?' He croaked. Suddenly my mouth felt dry, as I became nervous to ask any more, but the nagging curiosity inside got the better of me.

'Why do you have a copy of an article written by Mr Viton there?' I pointed toward the object on the desk.

Mr Brindle looked at the article curiously before slowly moving behind me. He made his way to his office door, pulled it to gently and I heard the clank of the metal lock being turned.

'Mr Brindle?' I said, apprehensively. It was as if something had overtaken the man, usually he would have just yelled at me or told me to mind my own business, but his strange demeanour was more sinister than I had ever seen before. Once he was sure the door was locked, he turned back to me, a grim look on his face.

'I think you need to start telling me the truth, Lee.'

I looked at him confused. 'What have I done?' I asked, genuinely puzzled.

Mr Brindle rubbed his eyes, as if he were tired. 'Mrs Brindle saw that rat, Viton in here before the party. What did you talk about?'

I gulped slightly and tugged at my collar. Mr Brindle was staring at me with a devilish intensity, it was as if just by staring he was raising the temperature within the room.

'Well…' I began nervously, 'he came in to ask me some questions about the Manor.'

Mr Brindle raised his eyebrows, nodding gently. 'Go on,' he said coarsely.

'He showed me some documents,' I replied.

'Ah. Let me guess, they show you who lived there before?' Mr Brindle said, pacing back toward his chair on the other side of the desk.

'Yes, they did actually.' I was surprised at his callous acceptance of this but felt wary of asking more. Mr Brindle lowered himself into his seat, his old bones creaking as he did so. He cleared his throat before saying:

'I suspect that you have some questions then.'

I nodded as a bead of sweat trickled from my forehead. Mr Brindle threw up his arms.

'Well, ask then. Or are you going to make me wait all day?'

I whipped my brow with my sleeve before daring to ask:

'All those people listed as living there. I don't remember any of them... but my name is on the paperwork, it seems like I showed them around. I want to know what's going on.'

My knee was bobbing up and down uncontrollably as I glanced back at the locked door nervously. The four walls of the office had now become my prison. Mr Brindle rubbed his hands together, as if thinking, before deciding to answer.

'The thing is, my wife and I, we killed those people, just like we killed Samantha Highcliffe.'

Normally I would have assumed this was a bizarre joke, but the sincerity and seriousness with which he spoke told me he was telling me the truth. I bolted upright, knocking my chair to the floor.

'What do you mean? Why would you do that?' I exclaimed, backing away slightly from the desk. Mr Brindle was shaking his head nonchalantly.

'It's not what you think,' he began, 'it wasn't for money or for pleasure or anything like that. We had to do it to survive.' He had this look on his face of hope that made it seem like he thought he might explain his way out of this situation.

'What do you mean survive? You aren't making sense!' I yelled back at him, angered by his callous outlook. Those were people he claimed to have killed, people with lives and hopes and dreams.

'Just sit down and we can talk about this,' Mr Brindle said calmly.

I backed toward the door, holding the handle tightly in my shaking hand.

'I'm not going to sit or calm down until you explain to me what's going on.'

Mr Brindle remained sitting and nodded acceptingly.

'Okay then.' He sighed. 'The truth.' Suddenly, he clutched at his head and tore at the skin, as if it were nothing but tissue paper. I watched in horror as the person that I had known to be the old, grouchy Mr Brindle was torn away, pieces of his face discarded on the floor, his body replaced by a shadowy being, spineless with two white hypnotizing, terrifying, enthralling eyes. I was frozen, unable to move, unable to look away, totally at the mercy of this beast before me.

'Now you see me as I am.' The voice that I had known as Mr Brindle's emanated around the room, despite the creature seemingly having no mouth.

'What are you?' I whimpered, but still stood like a statue.

'You couldn't comprehend even if I told you,' the voice rang out.

'Why did you kill those people? And why can't I remember them?' I said, a single tear falling from my horror-stricken eyes.

'Like you humans, we need to feed,' the voice explained coldly, 'for you, it is meat, vegetables, for us. We feed on something higher, something purer. Dreams.'

I was confused, 'Dreams?' It didn't make sense. But seeing the creature there in front of me, what did any more? 'But why do you kill a person then? Surely, they'd be better off alive, then they could keep dreaming.'

The creature wobbled and moved like a shadow flickering in the sunlight.

'I agree with you. If only it were possible. But sadly, our feasting process is too much for you… humans. It takes a toll on the body.'

I longed to move, to run, to be free, to forget all of this, but it was too late, I was ensnared and unable to escape.

'Why be Mr Brindle then? Why bother? Why not just be… that?' I said. There was a strange chuckle that further unnerved me before an answer came.

'You're just like my wife. She wonders why we bother. She loathes taking on these human forms. But I know the truth, to understand one's prey, you must act like one's prey. The more I grow to understand humanity, the better I can pick our targets, the more we can find those with the largest, tastiest dreams.' There was a sound that sounded like the smacking of lips, like having just been presented with a delicious meal.

'The truth is Lee. I've come to value my life as a human. The way you go about your lives, living the best you can, striving for a better tomorrow. I envy you. While you dream, we cannot. All we can do is feast and watch on. The thing I love most about you humans is that no matter who, big, small, poor, rich, man, woman, it doesn't matter, you all have dreams. Something about that is so innocent and pure, I can't help but long to be like you. So I live, as long as I can, as Mr Brindle, watching and learning.'

I had remained silent while the creature spoke, unsure of how to process this information. It felt as if my mind were being slowly screwed into a ball, then ripped and torn asunder.

'You still haven't told me why you have Mr Viton's article,' I said.

There was a slight sigh. 'Well, unfortunately, you sometimes get these people, who over the years have taken too much of an interest in our comings and goings. It's unfortunate, but they have to be dealt with.'

I gulped. 'Dealt with?' I barely dared to guess.

'Well yes, they can't interrupt our plans.' The creature shot back, as if irritated by the question. 'I hadn't planned on being rid of Viton so soon, I didn't like him snooping around, but I didn't think it would come to all that.'

It felt as if my whole body were going limp and I felt quite faint, yet my body remained upright. A chill shot through me, Mr Viton, was he... he wouldn't have killed him. Surely not.

'Still, I keep little trinkets of them. Something to remember them by, so that they're lives are remembered by someone, even if it's only me,' the voice continued and the creature opened a desk drawer, revealing an assortment of items and knickknacks, some old and rusting. Just how long had this all been going on?

'And now I'm afraid our time together is up,' the voice said, almost regretfully.

'Are you going to kill me?' I asked, my heart pounding, my body screaming.

The creature slithered toward me inhumanly. It's hypnotizing white eyes grew level with my own pupils, they almost reflected off the shimmering surface.

'I wouldn't kill you. I value you too much. No, you'll simply forget that's all. Forget what you've seen. Forget what you know. It'll be like waking from a dream – nothing but a hazy memory left in its place.'

Suddenly, something flashed into my mind, repeated images, myself with Mr Brindle, this exact scenario, repeated over and over. I finally understood, the curious Manor was a façade created by these creatures to lure in unsuspecting victims. It was like waking from a deep slumber, groggy, the pieces slowly moving into place.

'Have we had this conversation before?' my voice trembled.

'Oh, many times my friend, many times,' the voice said soothingly. 'Now relax, drift off to sleep, and dream that eternal dream.'

My eyes shut quickly and a warm, comforting darkness took hold.

***

It was a crisp spring morning and the sun was shining brightly through the window of our humble letting agents. Inside the office I could hear Mrs Brindle engaged in a one-sided shouting match with her husband and my boss, the grouchy Mr Brindle. She promptly stormed by as I hid my gaze within some letters. As she exited the shop and disappeared from view, I was called into the office of Mr Brindle. From behind a mountain of paperwork, he emerged with a furrowed brow. He explained to me that we had been sent a letter by a landowner and that we were to sell one of the most magnificent properties in the whole of Melford. I was to go and value the property.

The property in question was a Manor of some repute. You see, the curious thing about Ashbrook Manor was that no-one remembered it being built.